War Games

Jacqueline Guest

James Lorimer & Company Ltd., Publishers
Toronto

James Lorimer & Company Ltd., Publishers acknowledges the support of the Ontario Arts Council. We acknowledge the financial support of the Government of Canada through the Canada Book Fund for our publishing activities. We acknowledge the support of the Canada Council for the Arts for our publishing program. We acknowledge the support of the Government of Ontario through the Ontario Media Development Corporation's Ontario Book Initiative.

The Canada Council   Le Conseil des Arts
for the Arts   du Canada

ONTARIO ARTS COUNCIL
CONSEIL DES ARTS DE L'ONTARIO

Library and Archives Canada Cataloguing in Publication
Guest, Jacqueline
    War games / Jacqueline Guest.

(SideStreets)
ISBN 978-1-55277-036-8 (bound). — ISBN 978-1-55277-035-1 (pbk.)

    I. Title. II. Series.
PS8563.U365W37 2008   jC813'.54   C2008-904714-1

James Lorimer &
Company Ltd., Publishers
317 Adelaide Street West
Suite 1002
Toronto, Ontario, Canada
M5V 1P9
www.lorimer.ca

Distributed in the
United States by:
Orca Book Publishers
P.O. Box 468
Custer, WA USA
98240-0468

Printed and bound in Canada
Manufactured by Webcom in Toronto, Ontario, Canada in November 2010.
Job # 372721

In recognition of the struggles and triumphs of the families and loved ones of Canadian military personnel.

They also serve who only stand and wait.
– John Milton

Thank you to Corporal Jason Tabbernor, Princess Patricia's Canadian Light Infantry, 1st Battalion, for the invaluable help with the military details, and Stephanie Tabbernor, for the behind-the-scenes information only the wife of a soldier would know.

Chapter 1

Ryan Taber saw the sun glint off the rifle barrel as it slithered out of the second-floor window high above. His heart sped up as he realized this bombed-out building was where the rest of the Nomad fighters were hiding. He reloaded his weapon as he paused to plan his next move, and then kicked open the charred wooden door.

Noob — you suck! That's a fatal error, and now you're going to pay with your ass!

The taunting words appeared in the personal message box in the bottom left corner of Ryan's computer screen. *As if*, he thought, his eyes sweeping the scene for concealed Nomads. Nothing.

Then a hail of bullets rained down. He watched numbly as his avatar crumpled to the ground.

"Oh, man!" Ryan groaned. "I was two kills away from an Executioner rating."

The guy sitting at the next terminal looked over, assessing the carnage on Ryan's screen. "Let's see, that would mean right now you're a Lethal Hunter, and any *Desert Death* gamer with those stats ought to know better than to walk into an obvious ambush. You should have 'naded that top floor window and waited for the targets to bail out the front door. You could have registered a dozen kills." He nodded at the image. "From that slaughter, I'd say you made a real rookie mistake."

The insult stung. *Desert Death* was Ryan's game, and he lived for the thrill of hunting the ruthless desert fighters who disappeared into the sands, only to reappear locked and loaded. It was war reduced to the barest elements — you against the enemy. When he played, he was the boss at any level. Warrior Monk, his *Desert Death* alter ego, was a force to be reckoned with, and that made up for the rest of Ryan's life.

"Hey, I'm no raw recruit," he protested. "I've been playing since it launched. And I'm guessing you play *D-Death* too." Folding his arms, he sat back from his computer. "You're good at giving advice, but you haven't told me where you're at."

The newcomer scoffed. "I'm so far above you, it's a joke. Try Death Dealer."

Ryan's eyebrows shot up. "No way!"

"The higher the body count, the better I like it,"

the guy boasted. "The name's HacknSlash."

That was a name Ryan knew. It was legendary. This guy had smashed every record at the CyberKnights Gaming Café and was truly a cybergod. "Dude, you own this place!" he blurted, and then felt his face colour at the outburst.

"Yeah, you could say that." HacknSlash casually smoothed his blond hair back from his forehead.

Ryan nodded toward his terminal. "You sent the message."

"I decided you needed to sweat a little before the end."

Ryan took in the ace gamer with new respect. The guy was on the short side but looked muscled enough to be a boxer, and was wearing designer everything. High-end sunglasses were pushed up on his head, and he had a Blackberry Thunder sticking out of his pocket.

Suddenly self-conscious, Ryan was only too aware of his faded T-shirt and worn jeans with the pant legs too short. He was tall and skinny for fifteen and had trouble putting on weight, which made him look like a poorly dressed garden rake. Next to this guy, he could have passed for a bottle-picker.

"That message really messed with my concentration. I was totally creamed."

The gamer snorted. "Bots aren't smart enough to set a trap like that, so a higher power had to take over. I must admit you did a pretty good job."

"Pretty good" was serious praise from someone of HacknSlash's calibre, and Ryan appreciated the pat on the back. As for a higher power helping, if it would let him play like this master, he was all over that. "Thanks. Just remember, I was the one who ended up in the dirt."

The gamer shrugged. "If you hadn't screwed up by making yourself an easy target, it might have turned out differently."

"Maybe." He wondered why this guy, who obviously had money to burn, would play at a hole-in-the-wall café instead of having some elaborate setup at home. "I come here because my computer isn't fast enough. I don't remember seeing you around before, though."

CyberKnights was Ryan's favourite hangout. The dimly lit room was filled with the glow from a hundred terminals, and the blasting rock music was hard not to like. Everyone was focused on their game and there was little talking. It was a haven, and he came here whenever he had three dollars to spend.

HacknSlash stretched his fingers, cracking the knuckles loudly. "I've got an adequate setup at home, and only come here for kicks. I usually log on at night, but had some time this afternoon so I thought I'd drop by. I'm glad I did." He nodded at the two monitors. "That was great. Lucky we were assigned side-by-side machines, or we might never have met. I'm used to kicking ass in cyberspace and never knowing who I blasted." He eyed

Ryan's freshly cut hair, and the corner of his mouth crooked up. "You must be from the base."

"Yeah, Jason, that's my father, is with Princess Patricia's Canadian Light Infantry. And the new do," Ryan ran his hand through the super-short bristles, "is 'cause his battle group is leaving for Afghanistan tonight and we have to go to some send-off deal. He freaks if it's not chemo-patient short. I thought if I had to get scalped, I might as well treat myself to a reward, and this place is always my first pick." He swiped at the tiny hair bits that had settled in the frayed neck of his T-shirt. "My user name's Warrior Monk, but the outside world knows me as Ryan Taber."

"I think I'd tell my old man to get stuffed if he tried to make me get a buzz like that," HacknSlash taunted.

"Yeah, well, it's not so easy when you live with G.I. Jason." Ryan logged off the computer. At their house, two things were always in plentiful supply: overdue bills and discipline. His father was spit-and-polish old school, and that meant any kind of screw-up landed you an instant twenty push-ups or a hundred gut-crunches.

Thinking of Jason reminded him he was late and had to leave, although he would much rather have stayed and talked to HacknSlash about their mutual passion. "I gotta go. Maybe I'll see you around sometime."

The Death Dealer's face split into a grin. "That sounds good. It's not often I find anyone I consider even near my level. We should plan on another meet. By the way, the name out there," he nodded at the tinted windows of the café, "is Casey Ardmore." He began entering keystrokes at a frantic rate as he scanned his monitor. "Don't take any wooden Scuds."

Ryan felt like a kid at Christmas. He had met HacknSlash, and the guy wanted to get together again. Too freaking unbelievable!

As Ryan climbed on his mountain bike, he checked to make sure no idiot had dinged the Mongoose while it sat in the rack. Satisfied, he started for the Permanent Married Quarters on the base. He wasn't looking forward to the ceremony, only what followed — Jason flying away for seven long, rule-free months. All he had heard for weeks was a monotonous litany on how Jason was going to repair the wells of poor Afghan farmers so they could irrigate their crops and have clean water to drink.

Ryan stomped down on the pedals and his bike leaped forward.

They couldn't even eat in peace without some lecture detailing how ISAF, the International Security Assistance Force, would build schools so all the kids, even girls, would have access to an education.

He gritted his teeth and pumped harder, the wind stinging his eyes.

And then there was the one about the brave Canadian sappers, whose mission was to rid the countryside of the landmines left behind from pre-vious wars.

He wheeled onto the shortcut to the base. *Yeah, yeah,* Ryan had heard it all before.

To him, the idea of roaring around the desert in LAV IIIs, blowing things up sounded like the best adrenalin rush in the world. Still, Jason could be a real hard-ass when it came to playing soldier boy. His rules of engagement were strict: no dirty deeds and no illegal firefights, even if the target was sitting in your crosshairs.

None of that mattered. Before this day was out, old G.I. Jason would be marching off to war, and Ryan could hardly wait.

Chapter 2

Ryan's mother was watering her one sickly house-plant when he came through the door. Her hair was, as usual, pulled into a thick braid that hung to her waist. She had on the blue-and-white flowered dress that Ryan thought looked like something his gran would wear. All that was missing were the thick brown stockings and ortho-pedic shoes. It ticked him off to see her dressed so shabbily, and he wished she'd spend some of Jason's precious money to buy new clothes so she'd look more like the other moms.

She smiled warmly. "Well, hello, handsome stranger. What have you done with my shaggy-headed son?"

Ryan grimaced and watched her pick at the limp plant in her hand. "Honestly, I don't know why this violet won't grow. I water and water it, still the poor little thing's not doing so hot." She tucked it back out of sight on the shelf at the end of the cupboard. "Sit, sit. I'm about to put the food on the table. We'll eat supper quickly and then head over for the ceremony. You'll need to change clothes ..."

"Relax, Mom. Can I at least take my coat off?" As Ryan hung his jacket and sat, his father came into the kitchen. He was already in his uniform, the sergeant's epaulette precisely in the centre of his chest. Ryan thought the maple leaf with the three arrow-like chevrons looked like a neon sign saying, *Shoot Me Here!*

Jason Taber glanced at his wife, who was throwing several yellowed leaves into the garbage. "For pity's sake, Stephanie, toss that weed out. You know I don't like those things in the house."

Ryan's father was tall and very fit, with dark brown hair shaved close to his head. When he saw Ryan, his square jaw tightened in that rigid way that was all too familiar. "That's more like it, Soldier. A proper cut like that will be good for swimming. I made arrangements at the base pool for you to do lengths four times a week. You'll start with a mile, beginning at twenty-hundred tonight, then work your way up to five before I come back. It will pack some muscle on you, and you could use it." He eyed his son's lanky frame while Ryan squirmed under his scrutiny.

"I thought we talked about me taking guitar lessons. I've already looked into it." Ryan knew he sounded whiny, but this time he didn't care. Swimming was last on his list of great ways to spend spare time.

"No, *you* talked about it." Jason took his seat at the head of the table. "I said you had to do something more physical. Remember how you bombed when I took you climbing last summer? You didn't have the strength to make it up even the easiest rock face." His father looked disgusted. "You spend an unhealthy amount of time in front of computer screens playing those bloody war games. Thank God you got that fancy mountain bike. It might save you from turning into one of those soft delinquents who hang out at West Edmonton Mall."

At the mention of his bike, Ryan looked up. It was the coolest thing he owned and the only thing he and his father agreed upon. "It might," he said, with a hint of sarcasm slipping in.

His mother joined them, setting a platter of fragrant pork chops in the middle of the table. "Now, now, gentlemen, let's enjoy our meal."

His father took two large chops, then dished mashed potatoes onto his plate. "Remember, Ryan, I still want updates on how you're doing in school. You have a math exam coming up Monday and I expect to be apprised of your mark." He handed the potato bowl to his son before turning his attention to his wife. "Stephanie, change of plans. I have to head in early to make sure everything's a go. The Carters will pick you two up at seventeen-hundred, and I'll meet you at the assembly point at seventeen-twenty."

Ryan's mother looked crestfallen. "Oh, I thought we'd spend the time together before you leave."

"Captain Walstram asked me to check some last-minute details. The brass is counting on yours truly to ensure this goes off without a hitch." He cut his meat vigorously. "I'll make it up to you when I get back."

"Just come home safely, and all is forgiven." She smiled indulgently and Ryan saw his father smile back. He wondered if Jason's face hurt from forcing the rarely used muscles into action.

Ryan knew it was unfair, but he blamed some of the homegrown friction on his mother. She never complained, even though he thought she should. This made Ryan sound like a sniveller when he said anything negative. To keep peace in the family, his mom did what every good soldier should — she obeyed orders. And when Ryan and his father had a battle, she was there waving the white flag and trying to make a truce.

"And, Soldier," his father continued, "while I'm over there, it's your job to take care of the nuts and bolts around here. There are things you can do to keep the ship running smoothly, like helping your mother with chores and upkeep."

"I know, I know."

"No lip, young man. This is serious. Your mother can't do it all, and I expect you to step up."

Ryan didn't say anything as he jabbed his mashed potatoes with his fork.

***

The ceremony went off with military precision, of course. Ryan watched as Jason climbed onto the transport to the airport for the seventeen-hour flight to Kandahar Air Field where the main Canadian camp in Afghanistan was located. Everyone was waving insanely as they said their farewells. His mother's sobs started the second Jason's butt was on board the green military bus. Ryan, however, felt very differently as he watched his worries drive away. It was as though a magic door was opening and all he had to do was walk through to be in a whole other world, one in which he made the rules. It made him a little light-headed as he stood beside his teary mother.

When they returned home, he dutifully went to get his swimming gear, already planning how the Jason-engineered water torture could be modified to be more tolerable.

He poked his head into the living room and saw his mother. She looked as worn-out as the threadbare chair she was sitting in.

The military cared nothing for flash, and this was rigidly reflected in every corner of the Taber household. If it could be fixed, jury-rigged, or duct-taped together, they kept it. They didn't even own a car because Jason thought it was an unneeded expense. They didn't need to drive; they marched.

When he looked closer, he saw his mom's eyes were red and swollen. "Hey, you okay?" he asked hesitantly.

She sat up straighter. "Oh, hi, honey. Yes, I'm fine, just a little tired. It's been a long day. Are you off to do your laps?" She hastily wiped her nose with the tissue she had been clutching.

His mother's meek tone riled him. It was Jason's fault she was like this. He had volunteered to go on this tour, and didn't give one thought to those he left behind when duty called.

Ryan had to try to ease his mom's worry. After all, he was now the acting man of the house. He dropped his swim bag. "In a while. I thought I'd make a cup of tea first. Want one?"

His mother sniffed, then smiled weakly. "You must have read my mind."

Ryan made the tea he didn't want and sat drinking the cup he didn't need. He watched his mom as she sipped, and he hoped she would be able to cope with Jason gone. His mom had never seemed that strong.

"Everything's going to be fine," Ryan reassured her. "He's been dying to get over there and save the world. And you know G.I. Jason won't let anything upset his perfect plans."

His mother frowned. "Don't be disrespectful. We may not like it, but that's your father's job." She looked around the room as though seeing it for the first time. "I guess you and I are in charge of this operation now, Soldier."

"I'm sure we'll be able to handle the assignment." He gave her a mock salute and a genuine grin. "General Ryan reporting for duty, ma'am!"

She raised an eyebrow. "*General* Ryan? What does that make me?"

"Why, the Supreme Commander, of course — the General's *mother*!" He set his cup down, then stood and grabbed his bag. "Guess I better go. I wouldn't want to be late for my first session."

"Technically, Sunday is a school night. What time do you think you'll be home?" she asked, but he was already heading out the door.

Chapter 3

As Ryan sliced through the cool water he felt a tingle of exhilaration. Eyeing the lap clock to check his time, he felt like he was playing a video game. He concentrated on his stroke and tried to shave a millisecond or two off every lap. Finishing his mile, he was surprised to find himself so pumped. He hated to admit it, but Jason had been right. He could feel the muscles in his arms and chest burn from the workout, and it felt great.

Doing the mile had taken less time than he thought, which worked nicely with phase two of his plan, the part where he dropped in at CyberKnights for a quick game of *Desert Death* before going home. This would set the pattern for his mother. He didn't have to tell his mom he had added an hour of gaming to his swimming sessions. It would be his personal reward.

Ryan strolled into the café, signed up for a

computer, and was working his way through a Nomad stronghold when someone dropped into the chair next to him.

"Here to take out more bad guys?"

Casey Ardmore sat there smirking, bathed in the sickly green glow from the monitor.

"Hey, HacknSlash." Ryan wanted to seem cool. "What's up?"

"Funny you should ask, my man. I was about to do battle myself. Care for a little wager on who hammers who in the body count?"

Ryan still felt strong from his swim, and challenging a master like HacknSlash was exactly what he wanted to do. "You're on!"

They had been playing for nearly an hour when Casey sat back and announced, "I'm done here. You wanna go for a drive or something?"

Casey never mentioned that his kill count was way higher and Ryan decided that's what a real champion would do: he would never rub his opponent's nose in it. Unlike Jason.

Ryan wanted to take Casey up on his offer, but knew he should head home. He was already wondering how he could explain his long absence to his mom. Then he thought of G.I. Jason, winging his way farther and farther away, unable to issue orders any more. In his mind, the imaginary door beckoned again. It was time to step through.

He logged off the server. "Sure. No problem."

Casey's car was an expensive silver Mercedes CL 550 coupe with a seven-speed transmission.

Ryan had never been in anything more exciting than a second-hand Ford Tempo, and was impressed as they slid through the streets of Edmonton. Lights flashed by, landmarks were a blur, and the High Level Bridge winked patches of light and dark as they rocketed across. Ryan's adrenalin level rose with the speed.

Casey was obviously a risk taker. It took Ryan a fraction of a second to decide he wanted to be one too.

"This is what I call living," he said as Casey ignored a red light, barely making it across the intersection before a pickup truck barrelled through the opposite green.

"Yeah, look at all the little people. I could never be like the rest of the sheep."

"Sheep?"

"You know, all the good citizens who stumble through life never questioning the system, always following the same old rules."

Now there was something Ryan completely agreed with. Last report card, one of his teachers had called him *sullen*. The real problem was that the teacher simply bored him. School bored him. His life bored him. "That's exactly how I feel! Why live according to someone else's ideas? Why not come up with your own? The world is full of brain-dead … brain-dead …" He fumbled for the right word.

"Sheep?" Casey finished.

They choked with laughter and, for the first

time in his life, Ryan felt in sync with another human being.

After they had toured around for a while, Casey turned to Ryan with a smirk. "I have to pick something up. You in?"

Ryan wasn't about to quit on his new adventure. "Sure!"

They drove in twisted circles and bumped over railway tracks, stopping at a dilapidated house in a rundown part of the city. Windblown garbage skittered like frightened rats across a broken sidewalk. There were sheets strung across the windows and the place had an abandoned look to it.

What a guy like HacknSlash would want at such a dive, Ryan couldn't guess.

"Wait here," Casey instructed. He disappeared into the darkness behind the house.

Ryan felt uneasy as he sat in the expensive car. He was sure it looked like a target to whatever predator lurked in the shadows.

After a couple of minutes, Casey returned and tossed a small package behind the driver's seat.

"What's that?" Ryan asked.

"Nothing much. The Hag from Hell, as I fondly refer to my mother, bets the horses, and those are winnings from her bookie."

Horse betting was something Ryan knew nothing about. "Isn't that kind of betting illegal?"

"What? Off-track betting's been around in Alberta for years. This place is just way off-track."

Casey laughed as he pulled a U-turn and started back the way they had come. "So, where should I drop you? Are your wheels at the CyberKnights?"

Ryan felt uncomfortable. Casey obviously thought he was old enough to have his own car. He didn't want HacknSlash to know he rode a bicycle like some punk kid.

"Ah, yeah, you can drop me off. I've got to use the can first, so don't bother waiting."

Casey drove back to the 24/7 gaming café. "Not a bad way to waste some time. We should do this again."

"Yeah, that'd work for me." Ryan was so elated, he had a tough time looking casual as he sauntered into the building.

The second Casey's tail lights disappeared, Ryan left for home and the lecture he knew was waiting. Somehow, his bike didn't seem like such a sweet ride anymore, not after cruising in the Caseymobile.

He rolled in near midnight and found his mother in the living room.

"Thank God!" she said the second he slunk in the door. "Honey, I've been worried. You never stay out this late. What on earth happened?"

He tried to diffuse the situation by using a light tone. "Actually, I really enjoyed swimming. Just don't tell Jason. If I'd known it was going to be that much fun, I wouldn't have kicked and screamed so much." He pursed his lips and pretended to think on it. "Kicked, maybe, but there would have been very little screaming."

His mother wasn't so easily diverted. "I had no idea it would take this long. I'm not sure it's a good idea for you to be out so late four times a week."

Ryan knew he had better smooth things over before his mom went any further. "Oh, tonight wasn't the usual kinda thing. The mile took longer than I thought, and then I hung around the pool for a while, you know, trying to fit in with the guys. I guess I lost track of time. Sorry." The lie rolled off his tongue easily. He knew his mother didn't like the way he was always alone playing video games, and the part about trying to fit in with the swim crowd would please her.

"Well, I guess it's okay. Next time, please call so I can go to bed." She sighed wearily. "I have enough grey hair. Tomorrow will come early, so be sure to set your alarm."

As he turned to leave, Ryan noticed that his mother had moved her scraggly plant to the living room. It was in the middle of the window, perched proudly on a wicker stand he'd never seen before.

"Where'd the plant thingy come from?" he asked.

"Oh that." His mother's hands fluttered nervously. "I picked it up at a garage sale last week. What do you think? Will Violet like her new home?"

Ryan didn't know what to say. That his mother hid the plant stand until now was beyond strange, and he knew Jason would not be thrilled with the clutter. Then it dawned on him why his mother had done such a crazy thing — *Jason will be gone for a very long time.*

He laughed conspiratorially. "I think she will, Mom."

As Ryan climbed into bed, it hit him that he had completely forgotten the math exam the next day. It was a tough unit — algebra — and he should have studied. Then he thought about everything he and HacknSlash had done. He had never felt that free. What was bombing one lousy test compared to that?

Chapter 4

Everyday, Ryan's mother waited anxiously for her husband's call. She would watch the phone, insisting Ryan lower the volume on the TV in case she couldn't hear it ring; then she would check the computer, hoping that magic *New Mail* icon had popped up.

The walls were thin and Ryan heard his mother pacing when she couldn't sleep at night, the creak of the floorboards keeping her company.

Saturday morning, the phone rang and he heard his mother squeal with excitement. "Honey, it's your father!" she yelled up the stairs to him.

It was way too early and there was no way Ryan wanted to get out of bed to talk to Jason, but he knew there would be problems if he didn't. Afghanistan was ten-and-a-half hours ahead of them, so Jason's Saturday was pretty well shot already. Now he was ruining Ryan's.

Ryan dragged himself downstairs and sat in the living room while his mother relayed both sides of the very long-distance conversation. She asked about the weather — *it was sixty degrees and they drank litres and litres of water*; about the food — *not as good as hers, but nutritious and lots of it*; about his job — *he had several projects he was working on already*; and finally, was he safe?

She didn't tell Ryan what his father answered to that one.

"He wants to talk to you." His mom held out the phone.

Ryan reluctantly took the receiver. "Hi, how's work?"

"I'm rebuilding a school that was bombed by the Taliban. Speaking of school, what did you score on that math test last Monday?"

Typical — not, "How are you, son? I miss you, son." No, just cut to the chase. Ryan dreaded telling his father how badly he had failed, then realized that the worst G.I. Jason could do was yell, and that was nothing new. "I got a D. I guess I studied the wrong stuff."

The reply was strangely delayed because of the time it took for the satellite feed, which made it seem like his father had paused to take a deep breath before launching into his lecture. Listening to the rant, Ryan was tempted to hang up. Finally, Jason asked him to put his mother back on the phone.

Ryan handed over the phone and trudged upstairs.

A short while later, his mom cracked the door open to his darkened room. "Your dad asked about swimming, and I told him you really liked it and have been going as scheduled. He thinks, with your progress, you could be doing six miles by the time he gets back." Her tone grew serious and there was a catch in her voice. "He also said he's very disappointed about your algebra mark, and wants you to do a half-hour review every night for two weeks."

His father's reprimand stung, even second-hand, and Ryan decided that it was the last time he would tell Jason any details about school. "Fine. I'll do the stupid review. I don't have a life anyway. Is he going to call very often?"

"Every day, I hope, but it's limited to five precious minutes. We can e-mail all we want, though."

It took Ryan a nanosecond to see the upside to e-mailing Jason instead of talking to him directly. If Ryan e-mailed, he held all the control. "Mom, since the call is way more important to you, how about you talk and I'll e-mail? That way I can spend more time thinking up newsworthy stuff to tell him."

His mother considered the proposal. "That doesn't seem fair. Why don't you visit online for the day-to-day things, and if you have something exciting to tell him, then you get the entire five minutes for guy talk."

After their disastrous first foray into phone

communications, Ryan couldn't imagine telling his father anything. Jason would only criticize and suck all the life out of whatever Ryan shared. "Yeah, Mom, that sounds great."

The next morning, when Ryan checked his computer, there was an e-mail from old Jase waiting. His finger was poised over the delete button, but he decided that, since he really was in control, he could erase it any time he wanted. He read the message.

It sounded like G.I. Jason was having the time of his life.

Sunday, 06:24 — Morning, Soldier. I trust the remedial work I discussed with your mother will be done on schedule. The school we're rebuilding is progressing well, despite the mullahs angrily protesting plans to let girls attend. I've also started an irrigation project and am waiting for a new electric pump for the water well. I hope the generator can handle it ...

Ryan read on. It was mind-numbingly boring until he got to the part about the mortar attack.

We were shaken out of our beds last night as a swarm of RPGs slammed into camp. We grabbed our helmets and pants, in that order, ha ha, and then spent the night huddled in the bomb shelter.

31

Now, that was more like it. Ryan reread the section. In his mind, vivid images of bombs exploding and men scrambling for cover swirled in the caustic smoke of battle. It was like the ultimate game of *Desert Death*. The excitement must have been unbelievable. Instead of deleting the message as he'd planned, he opened a folder and marked it *War Games*, then dumped the e-mail into it.

Chapter 5

Lancaster Park High was a squat, drab, green building with not one ounce of curb appeal — which, Ryan supposed, suited a school on a military base. It was not his favourite place in this world, or any world for that matter. Unlike other army brats, who seemed to adapt easily to the moves and changes that went along with military life, he always felt like an outsider. Lately, the feeling had been worse. He sat at the back of the class, rarely volunteered answers, and generally tried to make himself as inconspicuous as possible. He was sure most of his classmates didn't even know his name.

He didn't care if he was always the one on the outside. He had the cyberworld. There, Warrior Monk was not only accepted, he was important.

The bell sounded as Ryan slid into his seat and yanked his Social studies binder out of his backpack. He could hear students around him discussing the latest news from Afghanistan, relaying stories about insurgent strongholds, IEDs, and the latest roadside bomb attack. Technically, he supposed it was eavesdropping, but he always listened to these details with interest. Life imitating game.

"Good morning, people," Mr. Gregorwich began, drawing their attention to the front of the room. "This is Chantal Roy, here from the base at Petawawa. May is late for a student to transfer, so I expect all of you to give her a hand getting up to speed."

Ryan stared at the new student. She was easily the prettiest girl he had ever seen. He was suddenly very glad her family had been transferred. The only empty desk in the room was across the aisle from Ryan, and he watched her glide down the row toward it.

She caught him staring, and smiled.

Ryan grinned back dopily, and then realized he must look like a perv. Hastily, he opened his binder, fumbling clumsily as a wad of papers fell to the floor. Groaning, he bent to scoop up the mess. So much for brilliant first impressions.

Chantal stopped beside his desk and he could feel her watching him.

"I can help," she said, crouching to gather up the scattered pages. She held out a magazine that had been among the mess. "You are a *cycliste*?" she asked, nodding at the cover of *Bicycle*

Canada. "I always wanted to learn. Sadly, I have no sense of balance." Her French–Canadian accent was strong.

"I do. Ride, I mean." He felt like an idiot tripping over his tongue. He was about to try again when Mr. G. called the noisy crowd to order and the opportunity was lost.

After class, he waited as the other students filed out, watching their newest classmate as she studied a map of the school posted on the wall next to the door. He took his time leaving and, as he hoped, she stopped him as he walked past.

"*Excuse-moi*, I am going to English class next and this map is *fou* — crazy! Could you show me where it is?"

She looked so helpless, Ryan knew he had to do what any Warrior Monk would and ride in to rescue this damsel in distress. Unfortunately, when he spoke, he sounded more like a noob than a hero. "Ah, English, right. It's a little tricky to find." He took a pen out of his backpack and traced the path she'd need to take, marking the English room with a big *X*.

She studied the drawing, a small frown creasing her brow. "This is a big school. Maybe I need GPS! I am sure that I will get it after some time. This is only my first day."

He coughed nervously. "I'm Ryan Taber and you're Chantal Roy." He realized too late that this statement made him sound even more like a dork. The one thing that saved him from total geekdom was that he pronounced her last name, *Rwah,* like the famous French–Canadian NHL goalie, instead of *Roy,* as the teacher had.

Her face lit up. "Yes. And you pronounce it perfectly!"

She checked the map once more, then shrugged apologetically. "I should go, in case that I get lost. Thank you, Ryan."

He watched her walk away, and only after she disappeared around the corner did it hit him. He should have offered to show her the way! He could have been her personal guide and walked her to the classroom. He really was an idiot.

Chapter 6

After the next class, Ryan swung by his locker to get a textbook. He couldn't believe his luck when he saw Chantal at a locker directly across the hall from his. Who was he to slam the door when opportunity knocked?

"Hey, Chantal, how's the first day going?" he asked in what he hoped sounded like a smooth, yet friendly, tone.

"It is confusing, but I think I'm getting it." She smiled and Ryan's stomach did a couple of acrobatic rolls. He desperately tried to think of some way to keep the conversation going, then noticed the binder in her arms. There was a news clipping slipped into the clear plastic cover. He scanned the headline: *Canadian Soldiers Injured in Attack on Terrorist Hideout*. She had drawn exclamation marks at the end of the line.

It was the perfect opening. "Ah, I saw some

streaming video of that assault. I can give you the website if you're interested," he offered.

"It is not necessary, I saw this clip also. *Sanguinaire*. Anyways, I don't think the newspaper did it justice." Her tone had a hard edge to it. "There is so much carnage that we don't react the way that we should."

Ryan was intrigued. Here was the best looking girl in school and, though there was a minor translation problem, it sounded like she was into firefights as much as he was. Here was something they had in common, something they could talk about.

At that moment the bell rang. He silently cursed the timing.

As though reading his mind, Chantal put her hand on the article. "*Merde*! Now, I must go. Maybe we can discuss this later?"

"I could take you to your next class," he offered, cleverly making up for that morning's missed opportunity. His confidence was building by the second.

"Oh, it is not necessary. I am in math with Madame Johnson, which should be …" she craned her neck to check the number by the door at the end of the hallway. "Yes, it is there. See you soon, eh?" She beamed one of her deadly smiles at him before walking away.

Ryan cursed under his breath. He had struck out again. Grabbing his book, he slammed his locker door and hurried to class.

At lunch, Ryan was outside eating in the warm May sunshine by himself when Casey rolled up in his Mercedes.

"Hey, Taber, ditch your classes and come play *Desert Death*. The Hag is raggin' on me and I need to get out of there."

Ryan hesitated. He had never cut classes before. Jason would have killed him. There was only one class left that afternoon. Still, if Ryan blew it off, there would be a call home. How would he explain that to his mom?

It was then that he saw Chantal making her way through the crowd. This was his golden chance to make it onto her radar. He was sick of never being noticed, never impressing anyone. In a heartbeat, he decided to continue his journey through that magic door. A new Ryan Taber was about to take centre stage.

Slouching into his best rock-star stance, he waited until Chantal was within earshot. "Yeah, sure, I'll cruise with you. I'm sick of this place and was looking for an excuse to bail on my next class."

Tossing his pack into the back seat, he climbed into the car, aware that Chantal was watching as they burned out of the parking lot. He hoped the extreme act wasn't lost on her. After all, cutting was something only a truly daring hero would do. He was now a man of action. As they drove toward CyberKnights, Ryan settled into his new persona. He felt like it suited him perfectly.

There was bound to be a few glitches living up to the new image, and he realized the first one waited at the café. "I've got a small problem," he reluctantly admitted.

"Yeah, what's that?" Casey asked.

"I don't have much cash on me." Ryan felt like a first-class loser again.

"Must be an epidemic. I don't either." Casey cut the wheels and turned down a side street. "As a matter of fact, I was about to fix that little problem."

They pulled into a pay parking lot and Casey got out of the car and walked up to the young guy in the booth. After a brief exchange, the attendant slid an envelope to Casey, who tucked it away in his jacket.

"What was that about?" Ryan asked as Casey climbed back into the car.

"He's a buddy of mine. I lent him some money a while back and, since we were in the neighbour-hood, I thought I'd collect."

When they got to the café, Ryan waited to be assigned a computer, and desperately hoped he had enough coin to pay for at least one hour of playing time. He pawed through his pockets for the $2.95 he needed.

Retrieving the envelope the parking attendant had given him, Casey pulled out several twenty-dollar bills. "If we're going to play, you need a

membership card with lots of time banked on it."
He waved the bills in the direction of the café
employee Ryan recognized as Eugene.

Eugene took the money, then gave the thumbs-
up. "With this much credit on your account,
Warrior Monk, you're good for about six months
playing at your current rate."

Eugene filled out a form and took Ryan's
picture, which was imprinted on the new membership card. Ryan stared at the card in his hand.
He couldn't stop the smile that spread across his
face. It was awesome. He had always wanted a
membership, but never had enough money to
make it possible. His smile quickly faded. "Look,
man, this is too much; I'll pay you back as soon as
I can."

"Don't be a jackass, Taber. I need a worthy
competitor, and you're it." Casey moved to the
computers they had been assigned and slung his
jacket over the chair.

When the familiar desert landscape appeared
on the screen, Ryan immediately felt stronger and
tougher; all his perceptions heightened as he
assessed the possible targets and ambush points
for both him and the Nomad fighters. This was
where he truly belonged — battling to the death
with an enemy who understood the meaning of
ruthlessness.

As he and Casey settled in to play, Ryan found
he had trouble concentrating. His focus wan-
dered, and HacknSlash, blasting away in his own

scenario, soon had a score that warranted his Death Dealer designation.

In fact, Ryan sucked so dismally, he felt he owned every spawn point in the game. He just couldn't focus on *Desert Death*. Instead, his mind kept replaying his last conversation with Chantal. He thought of some really great lines and wished he could do the whole thing over again.

"Crappity, crap, crap!" Casey cursed as he watched two men come through the door of the café. "Gotta go!"

Two surly looking guys, big enough to moonlight as Mafia leg breakers, walked up and down the rows of computers, scanning the gamers.

Casey grabbed his coat and made his way to the far end of the row. Ducking behind the last terminal, he moved stealthily to the front of the café.

Confused, Ryan logged off and quickly followed. "What's going on?" Before Casey could answer, the two guys spotted them.

"*Hey! Ardmore — get your ass back here!*" the bigger of the two yelled.

"Come on!" Casey called to Ryan as he fled out the door.

Ryan saw the thugs barrelling toward them and bolted after Casey, knocking over several chairs to slow their pursuers.

Once outside, he leaped into the Caseymobile, barely getting the door closed before they sped from the parking lot, the suspension bottoming out as they lurched over the speed bumps. Ryan tugged at the seat belt, trying to buckle up as the car slowed around a corner.

In the side mirror, he saw a black SUV rumble over the parking blocks and roar into the street after them. It was one of those high-end Cadillac Escalades with 400 horsepower under the hood he'd read about. This was going to be a fast ride and, he suspected, way too much excitement. He could feel his pulse thumping rapidly. Those guys were after blood, and Ryan didn't want to find out if he was part of the deal or not. "They're following us!"

"Following is one thing, catching is another," Casey growled as he downshifted the Mercedes and gunned it. The sleek car screamed through the streets as they careened around corners, and ran lights. Then Casey turned down a one-way street — the wrong way!

Cars swerved to avoid impending head-on collisions. Ryan was white-knuckled as Casey deftly picked his way through the honking traffic. "What's going on? Who are those guys?"

"Those bastards say I owe them a little cash. It's a lie. We have to lose them."

Ryan could see right away that this didn't add up; it had to be about something much bigger. Thugs like that wouldn't hassle you unless it was serious. "Casey, those guys are out for your head."

"It's all a huge misunderstanding. I paid them back on a small loan, then they jacked up the payout with some freakin' interest rate I didn't agree to. Now they want more. There's no way I'm caving, so I have to cut out. Have a little faith. I'm not the one who's done anything wrong."

Ryan felt a twinge of guilt. He had never met anyone like HacknSlash, and the first time their new friendship was tested, he was ready to throw in the towel. What did that make him? Sides had to be taken. "I believe you, man. Now, let's ditch 'em."

Casey cut hard left and dodged down a narrow side street, bounced into the intersection, turned right, and fired down a narrow alley. He finally came to a stop in the lee of a large dumpster, out of sight from the street.

Seconds slowly bled past as they waited, but the ominous SUV never showed.

"I think you lost them." Ryan sat back and took a deep breath, trying to calm his heart rate.

"Man! I thought we were done for." Casey punched Ryan on the shoulder. "That was totally cool, the way you didn't bail on me."

No one had ever said something Ryan did was cool. "You'd have done the same for me."

Casey laughed. "No way. I'd have cut you loose. This pretty face is way more valuable than your skinny white ass."

Ryan looked at him in surprise, wondering if he was serious. Then Casey grinned and Ryan realized he'd just lived, really *lived,* and was still here to tell about it.

When they were sure the coast was clear, Casey

put the car in reverse and slowly backed out of the alley. "I'm totalled. I'll take you back to your place."

Ryan thought quickly, remembering his bike was still at school. He didn't want to leave it in the parking lot where it could be boosted. "Drop me at the school. I have some stuff to do first."

As he biked home, Ryan felt weak and exhausted. The adrenalin had worn off and his legs were like rubber bands. He couldn't stop wondering what the creeps would have done if they had caught up with them.

Chapter 7

Ryan arrived home to an empty house, and was grateful for the down time. He needed a breather to recover. All that action had left him exhausted. The chase could have been lifted right out of a scenario from *Desert Death*.

He checked the answering machine to see if the school had called. The light was flashing and, when he hit the play button, sure enough there was the familiar voice of the counsellor busting him for cutting class. If his mother got this message, Jason would find out, and even with his father thousands of kilometres away, that would be a total disaster. Ryan would have to handle this himself. He thought of how he felt with Casey. Yeah, he was almost sixteen and he made his own rules. He hit the *Erase* button and sauntered upstairs.

Firing up his computer, he carefully dated and composed a note explaining his absence, citing some vague family matter. He printed it out and, with a previously untapped talent, signed his mother's name, then tucked the letter into his backpack for Mr. Gregorwich tomorrow. He had dodged a bullet on this one, and no one would be the wiser.

When he checked his e-mail, the telltale icon was sitting in the lower corner of his screen. He clicked on it. There was a message from Jason. After the usual boring stuff, it got way more interesting.

When we're inside the wire things are pretty secure, apart from the occasional rocket attack, but once we get in our LAV IIIs or the Bisons and head outside, that's a whole other ball game. Suicide bombers, snipers, ambushes, it's all out there waiting and you need eyes in the back of your head. The saving grace in this whole operation is the Afghan people. They're not giving in to the Taliban and we have to help. I know I can make a difference here, Soldier, and I'm damn well going to try.

Man, those Taliban cowards were so like the Nomad low-lifes he nuked it was weird. Ryan could imagine the troops rumbling through bombed-out towns in their LAVs, guns locked and loaded, artillery shells roaring across the sky. The noise of the exploding bombs and the smell of cordite would be a thrill for any soldier. He would love to be there, outmaneuvering the enemy.

"Ryan, are you home?" His mom called, interrupting his pleasant daydream.

"Yeah, in my room," he yelled back.

"Come down here, young man!"

It sounded like someone was in trouble and, since he was the only other person in the house, it wasn't too hard to guess who it was. He tried to think of something fast — he was sure his mother had somehow found out about his skipping school.

Slowly he walked downstairs, stalling for time. What could he do, what could he say? He strolled into the living room, hands in pockets, looking like the most laid-back guy on the planet. His mom had done what she always did these days: she had come in and immediately turned the TV on to CNN for news on the war. She looked different, and he couldn't figure out why. Then it struck him. His mother was wearing makeup! And he had to admit it looked good on her, in a momish way.

Now that he thought of it, there had been other changes recently. They had started getting the newspaper. His mom scoured the pages every day looking for tidbits or articles on Afghanistan. It was as if she couldn't get enough on that hole. And her first words let Ryan know that the changes would keep on coming.

"I called the school to give them my cell number. They said you'd left and that they'd phoned home, but I checked and the machine is suspiciously clear of any messages."

Cell? His mother had got a cell phone?

Before Ryan could process the new information, his mom gave him a hard look. "Care to explain why you cut class?"

Ryan tried to think of some logical excuse, and then inspiration hit him. It was so simple; it was genius. He'd *lie*, just as he did about his late return from swimming.

"Ah, actually, I felt mega-lousy and decided to leave school. Casey Ardmore, this friend I was with, didn't want me to be alone, so we went to his house. I threw up a couple of times and now I'm fine. It must have been some cafeteria food I ate. When I got home, I accidentally erased the message from the school. I was going to tell you about it, you just didn't give me a chance. Sorry, Mom." He sounded so remorseful that he almost believed the line himself!

His mother looked at him hard, then seemed to accept his improvised explanation. She sighed. "Why didn't you call? I could have come and ..."

"What, Mom, *walked* home with me?" Ryan interrupted. He knew this was a sore spot with his mother. The car they didn't have would have been useful in just such an emergency. "Look, I'm not your baby boy any more. I'm old enough to decide for myself what I need to do." He didn't mean to be rude, but he *could* take care of himself. It was time his mother cut the cord.

"Yes, you are," she agreed. "And part of being

an adult is treating others with courtesy and respect. So next time let me know what's going on and save us both a headache." She rubbed her temples, as though emphasizing the point. "Right now, we only have each other, Ryan, and I'm the one responsible."

There was a catch in her voice and he wondered if she was going to cry.

A sudden burst of volume from the TV caught their attention. The screen showed an armoured column under heavy fire. When the tag line identified the troops as American, Ryan's mother immediately refocused on him. "I have to see that things run smoothly." She rummaged in her tote bag, then handed him a small cellular phone. "This should help avoid any future problems. I've already put my cell number on your contact list so we can get in touch with each other if we need to."

Ryan was astounded. "About time the Tabers crawled into the twenty-first century!" He flipped it open and the screen glowed an inviting blue. He could hardly wait to call HacknSlash and give him the number.

"Are you sure you feel okay now?" his mother asked, reaching out a hand to feel his forehead.

"Yeah, yeah." He pulled away from her as he continued examining the phone.

"I'll call the school tomorrow and tell them you were sick and it was a communication problem," she motioned to the phone, "that will not be repeated."

Ryan silently agreed. He had to be more careful the next time, so this scene wouldn't be repeated. He was catching on fast. Lying to his mother was easier than he had expected, and it made things run way more smoothly. She believed everything he told her, was putty in his hands. He could toss his brilliantly forged note, he wouldn't need it after all.

A snuffling sound broke through the sound of the TV. What was that? It was then that he noticed the plastic carrier box in the entryway. Something was inside, and it was alive. "What's in there?"

"This is Ruff Cut, so named because she's a real diamond in the rough." His mom retrieved the box, setting it in the middle of the floor. "Which translates into 'she needs a little work.' I was at the vet's today and they told me Ruff is a stray who needs a home for a couple of days, so I offered to keep her. Poor thing was hit by a car and her little leg is badly banged up."

"You were at the vet? You got a dog?" One more thing out of left field. His mom bringing an animal into the house was major, and he was finding it hard to wrap his head around what seemed like a whole new reality.

His mother opened the carrier door and a small brown beast glared out at them. An ominous rumble accompanied the stare.

"Come on, Ruff. It's okay. I'll get you some yummy kibbles and water." Her voice was high and babyish, and very non-threatening. Still, the dog didn't move from the safety of the kennel. The only indication it had heard at all was the increased volume of the growls.

Ryan snorted. "If you offered me dry kibble and water, I'd be pissed too." He winced at his slip of the tongue and waited for his mom to comment on the language. To his surprise, she ignored it.

"Nonsense. Please go to the kitchen and get said gourmet snack for our guest. I'll try to coax her out."

Again, his world shifted. Maybe his mom was afraid to get on his case. Since Ryan was the acting male head of the house, he was kind of like Jason, and she never gave *him* a hard time.

This brave new world was becoming very workable.

Returning with the dog food he found on the counter, Ryan saw his mom in her easy chair holding the ugliest dog he had ever seen. She looked happy sitting there, and he wondered how she was planning to explain the furry refugee to Jason, even if it was for only a couple of days.

Jason! The afternoon flashed through Ryan's mind. If his mom told Jason about today's "illness," he was sure his father would immediately see through the smoke. There would be huge repercussions. It made him angry to think of how he always had to do the right thing — never break the sacred Taber commandments.

He had to do some damage control, and fast. "Hey, Mom. About this afternoon's stomach bug

— I really am fine, not worth mentioning. In fact, I plan on doing my lengths at the pool tonight. You know how Jason wants me to swim, and we wouldn't want him upset over anything happening here. Poor guy has enough to deal with without us exporting our problems to him," he hinted.

At the mention of Jason's name, his mother stopped fussing over the dog and her face took on a softer look. "Yes, I suppose you should go if you're up to it. Your dad always asks how the swimming's coming along. Don't you tell him about it?"

Ryan had made it a point to avoid anything but meaningless drivel in his e-mails, and his swimming was neither meaningless nor drivel. "I'll be sure to fill him in more."

By the time Ryan left for the pool, his mom was leashing the dog. She said she hoped that if she took it for a walk, it would pee on the grass instead of the carpet, which was apparently its preferred choice of latrines.

The swim went better than any previous sessions, and Ryan found that his lap times were getting progressively shorter. His muscles didn't hurt any more. In fact, he felt stronger than he had ever felt as he kept up his blistering pace. A group of guys watched him finish his two miles, and as he headed to the showers, he decided he could have passed for a jock. What a concept!

Chapter 8

At school the next day, Ryan looked for Chantal. He was disappointed to discover they shared only their first class. He had wanted to get her phone number so he could put it in his cell's contact list; so far he hadn't even worked up the courage to stand beside her.

He dawdled as he left school in the hopes he would "accidentally" run into her. When it became obvious she wasn't going to show, Ryan walked over to the rack where his bike sat gleaming in the late afternoon sunshine. His cell phone jangled in his backpack.

His eyes swept the school grounds, hoping for an audience as he smugly took his first call. "Hello," he said, a little too loudly.

"Hi, honey, I'm going to be a little late and wanted to let you know I left supper in the fridge."

"Sure, Mom, I'll see you later. Bye." He

snapped his phone shut. His first call and it had been from his mommy.

The phone jangled again and Ryan wondered what chores his mom had forgotten to assign. He retrieved the phone and flipped it open without looking at it. "Yeah, I know, wash my dishes."

"Whoa, okay, but don't do anything fancy for me, man."

It was Casey, the only human on the planet besides his mother who had this number. "Oh, sorry, I thought it was someone else. What's up?"

"I have a bit of a problem and was hoping you could help me out."

Ryan heard the note of urgency in Casey's voice. "Sure, what do you need?"

"Do you remember that house we went to when we picked up the old Hag's track winnings? Do you think you could swing by there and grab another bundle of loot for my dear nagging mother? I can't, I'm seriously jammed up."

It was a long way, but Ryan knew Casey thought he drove a car. His friend was asking for a favour, and Ryan couldn't let him down. "Yeah, I can do that. It will take me a while, though. Where do you want it delivered?"

"Bring it over to my place."

Ryan wrote the address on a scrap of notepaper. It wasn't in the best part of town and he wondered if he had heard right. From the car Casey drove and the way he dressed and threw money around, Ryan assumed the Ardmores were doing better than all right.

After what seemed like a million miles, Ryan wheeled onto the street where the derelict house sat leaning into the wind like an old vagrant caught in a sudden storm. He parked his bike, went around back as he'd seen Casey do, and banged on the beat-up, old screen door.

The man who answered was straight out of a bad B movie. He was big, ugly, and decidedly unfriendly. He had what Ryan imagined were prison tattoos on his bulging forearms, which added to the menacing look of the dirty biker-gang vest. The foul smell of decay with an acrid undertone wafted past the open door.

"I've come to get a package for Casey Ardmore," he squeaked nervously. He grimaced at the sound of his voice. He was a man of the world now, accomplice of HacknSlash, the most feared Death Dealer in all of cyberspace. He shouldn't sound like a wimp.

The man grunted, then retreated into the dank recesses of the house. He returned with a small box wrapped in brown paper and sealed with duct tape, which he handed to Ryan.

Before Ryan could say thanks, the surly man slammed the door shut. "Nice talking at you too, moron." He stuffed the package in his jacket and started for his bike, but hung back around the corner of the house as a black SUV drove slowly by on the deserted street. Recognition flashed, then fear, as he remembered the last time he had seen the Escalade and the two burly men inside. Ryan knew they were looking for him. He waited for the SUV to pass, then bolted for his bike. Adrenalin spiked in his blood as his legs cranked hard on the pedals. He glimpsed brake lights flashing, then the swing of the bulky truck as it made a U-turn. He'd been spotted!

Years of gaming had honed his strategy skills, and now he was drawing on those abilities to keep ahead of his pursuers. He kept to the bushes and trees, using all the cover he could while pumping up his speed.

Because he was on a bicycle, he had way more options than the three tons of steel chasing him. With a nimble swoop, he split the lanes then dodged in front of the slower moving traffic as horns honked and curses from ticked-off drivers trailed after him. Well played, he congratulated himself, confident that having half-a-dozen cars as interference would stop the goons cold.

Ryan's confidence faltered as the light at the intersection up ahead went amber. He swore as he saw the SUV dodge his vehicular obstacle course and close the distance between them again. Pushing harder, he caught the late orange and smiled, sure he was home free this time.

A quick check over his shoulder changed his mind. He saw the big black tank barrel through as the light went red. They were reeling him in and he was out of options.

Imagining he was pinned down in a *Desert*

Death battle scenario, Ryan felt his pulse pound in his ears. Ahead, he saw a last chance to evade the thugs once and for all. It was a railway crossing and the lights were flashing their warning. Leaning low over the handlebars, he pushed for all he was worth.

The locomotive's horn blasted, shrieking at him to turn away. The train loomed above him, a giant metal monster from a bed-wetting nightmare.

Ryan had run crossings before, but never with this slim a margin. He could feel his muscles screaming as he used every last ounce of energy to beat the oncoming train. Behind him, he heard the Escalade's engine throttle up. At this velocity they wouldn't just stop him: they'd shove him under the train's grinding wheels!

Ryan could see his way to safety on the other side of the tracks. All it would take was a two-second window for him to make it. He took a deep breath and lunged for that window.

It was so close, he could feel the hot air rushing up at him as the train thundered by. He looked back and saw the SUV waiting.

He had to keep moving. Ahead of him, he saw the skeletons of half-built houses rising from a deserted construction site. He raced for it. Bumping his bike across the rough terrain, he crossed the site and blasted into the road on the far side. He turned down a blind alley and skidded to a stop behind a line of garbage cans.

Ryan laid his bike on the ground and crouched, watching and waiting. He tried to slow his jack-hammering heart as he took several deep breaths. His senses were on overload as he listened for his pursuers, but the only thing he heard was the rustle of mice feasting.

Something was totally whack. Why had those guys chased him? They had to know a kid on a bike wasn't Casey. Were they after the money? And how much money? He pulled the package out of his coat and had a bad feeling as he looked at it.

What if this wasn't track winnings? What if it was something worth hunting him down for, like drugs — serious in-your-veins drugs? He had to find out what was going on. Ryan picked at the edge of the sticky tape wrapping the box. Working carefully, he pulled until the brown paper was free. If this was drugs, he wanted no part of it. Holding his breath, he lifted the lid.

Inside, nestled side by side, were two neat stacks of bills — tens, twenties, and even some fifties. It was just as Casey had said. Winnings from a bet. He rewrapped the box, making sure the tape was well sealed. He shouldn't have doubted his friend. Ryan relaxed. The chase tonight had been a thrill ride and maybe he'd pushed it a little farther than he should have, but now that it was over, he felt like laughing. What a rush!

Ryan still felt the last edges of the excitement tingling in his body when, finally, he stood in front of the Ardmore's weathered house and rang the bell. The siding was faded and the basement windows were boarded up with plywood. It had the air of a place way past its best-by date. There was a high-tech closed-circuit camera by the door watching him. He waved the package and grinned.

Casey threw open the door. "Thanks, Taber. I owe you big time." He looked into the driveway and saw Ryan's bike gleaming in the last of the evening's light. "You're BS-ing me! You *pedalled* your ass all the way over here?"

The grin on Ryan's face faded and he shrugged, embarrassed, as he handed over the box. "Yeah. You said you needed help. I also had to lose those two creeps from the café."

"And you did all this on two wheels?"

Ryan didn't answer.

Casey checked out the bike again and nodded approvingly. "You are *the man*!" He slapped Ryan on the back, then went inside, gesturing at Ryan to follow.

Ryan felt elated at the compliment. He followed, then was immediately taken aback at the seediness of the place. The floors had missing tiles and the walls were in worse shape than the PMQs. He noticed a video monitor on the wall and guessed this was what the closed-circuit camera was slaved to, then decided it was overkill. From the look of the place, there was nothing worth stealing. Maybe some of those winnings he had brought should be used to give this dive a facelift.

"I'll ditch this and then bring you a beer." Casey tossed the package in the air, caught it, and sauntered off.

From somewhere out of sight, Ryan heard music playing. As he waited, he remembered HacknSlash saying he usually played from home and wondered what system the cyber king used.

"Hey, dude, mind showing me your setup?" he asked as soon as Casey returned.

"No problem. Right this way." They walked down a dimly lit hallway to a darkened room.

There were dual Alienware computers, two twenty-inch widescreen displays, trick gaming keyboards, and — from the hum that vibrated his back teeth — what Ryan guessed was a killer surround sound audio system. It was a gamer's paradise. "Sweet!" was all he could manage.

"Yeah, I know. The thing is, to keep up with my fave MMOs, I have to upgrade soon. Hey, you could buy my old stuff. It runs at warp speed, and I'd cut you a good deal."

Ryan had dreamed of a system half as great as this one, and then realized that in his dreams was as close as he'd ever get. "Sure, maybe," he mumbled noncommittally, knowing this system was worth mega-bucks, even used.

They walked into the living room, where music was thumping the walls and three guys sat on worn furniture drinking and laughing. Casey indicated a cracked leather chair as he left the room. "Have a seat." He returned with two beers.

Ryan had been musing about Chantal, but then he saw the beer and his mind switched gears. He could tell this crew had been drinking for a while and, from the trash talk, he wasn't sure it was a good idea to try and catch up. "Ah, maybe I better not. I have to ride home."

"Lighten up, my man." Casey shoved an icy bottle into his hand. "You earned it."

The magic door flashed and Ryan decided: *Why not?* "Okay, it's not like I'm driving, right?"

Chapter 9

Morning, Soldier. Lousy news. The Bad Guys burned down the school we were rebuilding. Mullahs said if we were going to let girls attend, it should be destroyed rather than allow such blasphemy. The next night it was fire bombed. What a waste. Things have tensed up outside the wire. Many more reports of insurgents targeting our patrols. The captain says we'll set up an extra checkpoint further from our perimeter to try to stop suicide bombers. We had an emergency and had to go out on a night operation. Nights are the worst.

Ryan held a cold, damp cloth to his head as he read his latest e-mail. He should have said no to those last two beers. It had been a late night, and he had gone straight to his room so his mother wouldn't smell the alcohol on his breath.

He could see Jason yelling at the mullahs for torching his school, then making them drop and give him twenty. *Yeah, right!* When he read of the night operation, he was there. He thought of his own op. Playing hide-and-seek with those goons had been wild. Jason had been sending lots of info on his lame projects, but the parts Ryan lived for were the firefights. He could imagine what it must be like to roll through the villages, king of all you surveyed.

His head pounded uncomfortably as he walked downstairs, and it nearly exploded when he stepped into the bright kitchen. He squinted at his mother, then stopped dead in his tracks and stared.

"Whoa, what happened to your hair?" Gone was the long braid Ryan had known all his life.

"After all the money I spent, I would have thought it was obvious, even to a boy. I got it … cut! Do you like it?" Her hand touched the short bob tentatively, as though confirming what she'd done.

He didn't know what to say. She looked so different — younger and, well, stylish. She had on a blue smock with small, brightly coloured puppies scattered across it. "And what's with the Wal-Mart greeter outfit?"

"It's part B of my surprise. Remember I was at the vet clinic the day I brought Ruff Cut home? The reason I was there was to apply for a job. They were looking for a kennel technician, which is a fancy name for pooper-scooper/dog-walker, and I thought even I could do that." Her face was alight as she went on. "Don't think I'm abandoning you, Ryan. It's only part-time to start, so I won't be away long hours." The light suddenly drained from her face. "It turns out I have a lot of free time on my hands, and being busy helps. Besides, heaven knows we can use the extra money, and I can take Ruff Cut with me."

Ryan was stunned. "Let me get this straight. Jason is gone for a few weeks and you bring home a dog, cut your hair, and get a job. Oh, and buy a couple of cell phones!" He'd almost forgotten that detail. "And what did dear old G.I. Jason say when you told him all your news?"

His mom ignored the question and busied herself putting two slices of bread into the toaster. "You forgot to mention that I moved Violet," she added. Ryan could have sworn the corners of her mouth twitched.

His head was splitting open and she thought this was a joke. Rage welled up inside him. "Do you think this is funny, Mom?" he shouted. "He'll go nuts when he finds out and, you can bet your ass, life around here will go in the toilet! And do you know who he'll take his frustration out on? It sure as hell won't be you!"

Startled, Ruff Cut scuttled under the table, whimpering as though she expected blows to rain down.

His mother stared at him in shock. He had never spoken to her like that before, but this was serious. Jason was going to flip out. He saw a guilty look flash across her face. "You're kidding! You haven't told him, have you?" He ran his hand through his short hair. "Great, just great! That means I'll have to watch every word I tell him. You should have checked with me first."

Her face took on an expression he had never seen before. She set her lips in a firm line as she pushed her chair away from the table and slowly stood up. "That's quite enough, young man! It's not your decision what I do. *This is not Afghanistan and you are not the male head of the house.* Don't ever forget that, Ryan." She strode out of the kitchen. With a nervous backward glance, the dog followed her.

Ryan's panic started to ebb. This was so out of character for his mother. Maybe she was having some sort of breakdown because Jason was gone and there was no one to hold her hand. Whatever was going on, he doubted the ending was going to be happy. He had heard his mom laughing on the phone when she and Jason yakked, and had assumed everything was great. Maybe she did have to face a lot of empty hours. So what if she got a job?

He figured the angles that would work for him. His mom would have a guilt thing going at not being upfront with Jason, and involving Ryan in the scheme would add to that guilt. Looking after a dog, the usual household routine, and managing a new job would keep her so busy, she wouldn't have time to check into his business. It was all good.

***

School the next day was a total bore, but things looked up in a big way when Ryan saw a familiar figure at the bulletin board in the front hall. He pumped up his confidence, then walked over and scanned the flyer Chantal was posting.

"Hey, what's this about?"

"I am starting an information pamphlet to keep students up-to-date on everything that is going on *over there*."

She didn't need to say where *over there* was.

She brushed her hair back and went on to explain. "Everybody, they gossip and have bits of information, and I think it would be good if all the horrible statistics were verified so we know the truth." She looked at him sheepishly. "I also receive extra credit from Mr. Gregorwich, which helps, no?"

"Which helps, yes! Getting Mr. G. to give up a few more marks is usually impossible!" He was totally on track with her. "I like the idea of having the scoop on exactly how many Taliban bit the dust."

She looked confused. "I will post the number of casualties for both sides. I have a special section for civilians. They must not be forgotten."

"Oh, yeah, I agree, but collateral damage happens. That's part of winning the war." He was really getting into it now.

"Sometimes the costs are too high, and we need to look at the whole image again. Maybe change the way we win that victory."

Ryan frowned, taken aback. "There's nothing wrong with Canada's battle tactics. Sure, we're building schools and wells and all that crap. That stuff doesn't happen easily, though. It's two steps forward, one grenade back. The enemy has to be swept out of their holes first so our guys don't have to worry about bullets flying."

"*Absolument*!" she agreed. "It is critical that our troops work in safety. But don't you find it strange that safety is even an issue when all that our soldiers are trying to do is make things better for these same people who pose the threat?"

Ryan had never thought about it like that before.

She stacked a bundle of pamphlets on the desk under the bulletin board. "See you in class with … what is it you call him? Oh yes, see you in *Mr. G.'s* class." And with that she walked away.

Chapter 10

Ryan spent as much time away from home as possible to avoid listening to his mother go on giddily about her great new job. Instead, he made good use of his membership at CyberKnights. With all the extra practice, his rank had climbed to Executioner, and now he had his sights set on Terminator. He had stopped trying to make excuses to his mom about where he was or why he was late. He figured that if she could break all the rules, so could he.

Jason's section had gone on a long patrol, and neither Ryan nor his mother had heard anything in several days. Ryan liked not having to e-mail every day, but did miss the intense descriptions of the battle action. His mother would sit by the phone for hours and wait, which Ryan saw as a total waste of time. When old Jase got back from whatever *Save Afghanistan* project he was on, he'd call.

When the e-mail finally did come in, Ryan read it a couple of times. It was as though his father were talking to a grunt newly arrived on his first tour.

Listen up! Here are some rules to live by when you're over here, so carve them in stone.
Rule Number One: Don't trust anyone. Even children can be walking bombs.
Rule Number Two: Watch out for snipers. Never slack off because it will cost you or your buddy standing next to you.
Kalashnikovs have such a recognizable sound.
Rule Number Three: Nothing is what it seems. That baby buggy could be loaded with gelignite.
And Rule Number Four: Don't forget to pray.

Ryan shook his head. The e-mail was big-time out there. Jason had a brass ass when it came to the military protocol, but this was over the top, even for him. The part about the Kalashnikovs was very cool, though. Ryan wondered what one sounded like.

***

The following week, Ryan was at the café booting

up his usual computer when Casey sat down next to him.

"So how's it hangin'?" Casey asked.

"As a matter of fact, I'm about to leap into the stratosphere. Tonight, I go for Terminator."

Casey raised his eyebrows. "You think?"

"I know. Care to watch the bloodbath?"

"Ah yes, my favourite kind of bath." The Death Dealer leaned back, his hands clasped behind his head.

Ryan cracked his knuckles exactly the way HacknSlash did, and opened the game.

The fighting was brutal, and the concentration needed to evade the enemy was at an all-time high. HacknSlash offered advice as Ryan blasted his way through hordes of saboteurs, booby traps, and assassins disguised as crippled old men. "Nuke that kid!" he yelled.

Ryan's finger hesitated over the trigger. The little girl on the screen couldn't have been more than five years old. "She's a civilian!"

"So, you lose a couple of points for wrongful death. It's better than having your ass blown up by the C4 she has strapped to her body. Now, take her out! If she's a Nomad, you win, man!"

Ryan didn't play that way. He was discriminating about the people he mowed down, even if they were just characters on a computer screen. If the kill target was an ordinary citizen, you were penalized points for wanton violence and wrongful death. It was called an *Ethical Rating*, and the machine decided if you were a nice guy or not: if your ER was high enough, the game cut you some slack in certain situations, like having a convenient foxhole appear when you needed it most.

Ryan had his own code of conduct, and randomly killing anything that moved wasn't part of it. But HacknSlash was the master, and who could argue with success? Ryan focused on the child and squeezed the trigger. The tiny figure exploded as the bullet ripped through the explosives.

"Hey, Casey, you were right!" he laughed. The screen flashed, blinking the long-sought message proclaiming Ryan's promotion to the prestigious designation of Terminator. He was now only one rank lower than HacknSlash! "Thanks for the tip!"

"Don't let your head swell up too much," Casey laughed. "It makes it an easy target."

Ryan marvelled over it as he rode home in the soft evening light. He was officially a Terminator. He had wanted it badly, tried his hardest, and yet the prize had always slipped through his fingers at the last moment. Well, not tonight. He'd done it.

He wanted to call someone to share his triumph. The someone who immediately came to mind was Chantal Roy. He really wanted to be closer to her; in fact, getting closer was now his top priority. He would need to come up with a battle plan to help things along. A Terminator should be able to do that, no sweat.

The next morning, he woke still feeling euphoric and bounded downstairs to find his mother in the living room. "Hey, how's my favourite mom?"

"Well, good morning. My, aren't we in a good mood." Stroking the top of Ruff Cut's head, she scrutinized the room. "I think our living room looks kind of shabby. It needs sprucing up."

Ryan looked around. It seemed okay to him. Same faded green walls and gross brown water-marks where the ice had backed up under the shingles and then melted, staining the ceiling.

"So, tomorrow I have the painters coming in very early. Can you help me move the furniture and cover it tonight?"

Ryan stopped, his good mood evaporating. Another change to the status quo. Would his mom never learn? Maybe it wasn't too late to head off the inevitable explosion when Jason got home. "Are you sure you want to do that, Mom? Seems kind of extreme to me."

"Absolutely! And I don't want to hear another word about it. Now are you in, Soldier?" She stood up, energized with the prospect of this new suicide mission.

Ryan didn't have the breath to waste on her if she wouldn't listen to reason; he had bigger targets in his sights. "Yeah, yeah, okay. I'll help you after swimming tonight." A thought occurred to him and he had to ask. "Isn't this going to cost a lot? I thought money was always close to non-existent in this house."

His mother's chin came up. "I'm working now,

and Dr. Samson says I'm doing so well, she wants to train me on the counter. That means more responsibility, and with that comes more pay." She beamed, looking years younger. "A promotion, Ryan — my first promotion, and a pay raise to go with it." She pondered the room once more. "I'm thinking a lightish shade of cappuccino with cream accents, maybe crown moulding."

Shaking his head, Ryan left his mom to her mental consult with Martha Stewart and went to school.

Chapter 11

"Man, this is the life." Ryan leaned back and stretched his legs as the Caseymobile cruised through busy streets on their way to a cash pickup. He rubbed his calf, which had a minor cramp left over from his swim. He had finished his laps early and Casey had picked him up so they could hang out before he had to move the lousy furniture.

They pulled to the curb in front of the ruined house. "Come on," Casey said, jumping out of the car. "You've been picking up the Hag's winnings a lot lately, so I thought I'd introduce you properly to our neighbourhood bookie."

The battered door opened and the biker glared at them. "Vince, this is my good buddy, Ryan Taber," Casey told him. "Remember that name. He's been helping me out by doing the pickups, so I thought I'd introduce you all official-like."

"Hey, Vince." Ryan felt like he was truly one of

the 'leet now. HacknSlash had introduced him as a friend, and that meant something.

Vince grunted unintelligibly, turned, and disappeared into the recesses of the house.

"Whoa, I've got a call. Grab the cash, will you?" Casey retrieved his cell phone as he stepped away from the door.

The mangy biker returned with the package of winnings and handed it to Ryan.

There was a click and Ryan turned to see Casey tucking his phone in his jacket. "Let's head over to the café. I'm feeling like a game or two. Oh, and don't worry about burning your own credits, I'm picking up the evening's tab."

As they rocketed to CyberKnights, Ryan realized that since he had met the master gamer, things were finally going great in his life.

At the café, they went head-to-head. Again, HacknSlash pulverized Warrior Monk. Ryan was learning a lot about ruthlessness, and his own skill level had inched upward.

"Let's go to my house. I'm starved, and the garbage they have here sucks." Casey was already shutting his computer down.

Ryan was doing well and didn't want to quit the game. "Don't bail yet, man. I'm kicking Nomad butt."

"No way. Come on. *Now*!"

Casey grabbed his coat and was heading for the door before Ryan could voice any more complaints. A sliver of anger, sharp as broken glass, sliced through Ryan. Then he logged off and followed his friend.

When they got to Casey's, they ordered out and were finishing both the pizza and their second beer when someone pounded on the door. Ryan could see on the closed-circuit monitor that it was the same guys who had been there the first time he had been to Casey's place.

"Now we party!" Casey laughed and went to let them in. Before Ryan knew it, the music was blasting and the place was rocking.

The guy called Red rolled a joint and offered Ryan a hit. Casey was watching and Ryan knew this was some kind of test.

"Right on," Ryan said nonchalantly, taking the joint carefully and inhaling the bitter smoke deeply. His lungs burned and his eyes watered, but he held it in.

Everything went off the rails from there. The music got louder and Ryan's world became wilder. The room tilted and slid sideways as he flopped onto the couch. He sat perfectly still to keep the nausea from rising in his gut. Across the room, he noticed Casey and Red laughing as the two made an exchange of what Ryan assumed was yet another joint.

Casey spotted him sitting on the couch, waved, and grabbed more beers before heading over. Ryan had serious trouble focusing as he bobbed his head toward Red. "Man, you'd think your buddy would have had enough." His tongue seemed thick and his hand wavered as he reached for another beer.

"Not that animal. Ol' Red's cranking up the crank." Casey's words were slurred.

At first Ryan couldn't make sense of what he heard, then it coalesced in his muzzy brain and he clambered unsteadily to his feet. Booze and a little weed was one thing; crystal meth was a whole other ball game. He shook his head, causing the colours in the room to bleed together. "I have to go. Can you give me a lift back to the café?"

Casey looked at him with dilated pupils. "No can do, bro. It would be very impolite for the host to cut out right at the good part."

"So what am I supposed to do? Walk?"

Casey grinned drunkenly. "I could find you a bike and you could pedal your ass back home!"

With blurred vision, Ryan took in Casey, Red, and the rest of the posse. His temper boiled and he knew he had to get out of there before he lost it. "Later," he said curtly, as he stumbled out the front door.

When the fresh air hit him, Ryan took a deep breath and started coughing. His stomach lurched and he puked in the bushes at the edge of the driveway. Moaning, he felt like the Grim Reaper had come, taken one look at him, and decided he wasn't worth the effort.

By the time he picked up his bike from the pool and made it home, his head had cleared a little. Climbing the stairs to his room, Ryan tried to

78

make as little noise as possible. He fumed at Casey for getting him in that deep and then bailing. How could the guy treat him like that?

The next morning, he was hauled out of sleep by a pounding on his door. "Ryan, get up! The painters are coming in fifteen minutes."

Painters? Oh, man, he'd forgotten about the painters and his promise to help his mother. Had that really been only yesterday? The prospect of moving furniture made his skull pound. "Yeah, yeah, hold on," he croaked.

Groaning, he dragged himself out of bed. His eyelids felt like sandpaper. The second he tried to stand, his stomach twisted violently and he ran for the bathroom. With an excruciating effort he managed to slosh water on his face and brush his teeth to get rid of the foul taste in his mouth before pulling on his robe and gingerly making his way downstairs.

His mother was in her ridiculously cutesy uniform waiting for him. Instead of the expected lecture, she breezed on like everything was cool.

"I guessed you got hung up at the pool again, so I moved the furniture myself."

He took in the furniture neatly piled in the middle of the living room and draped with plastic. Something about it made him angry. Then it dawned on him. "So, you didn't really need me to move this junk. You wanted me home so you'd know where I was, so you could keep tabs on me!"

His mother stared at him blankly. "I don't know

where that came from, mister, but it sounds pretty silly to me. This *junk* is heavy." She shook her head, dismissing Ryan's accusation. "The painters will be here shortly. It's going to take them a couple of days to finish, so the house will be upside down for the duration. I'll get them started while you dress, and then maybe we can grab a bite of breakfast at the coffee shop before I go to work. My treat."

The idea of sitting with his mother while she ate greasy food from the local squat-and-gobble made his stomach rumble ominously. He couldn't face that horror show. His fuzzy brain dredged up an excuse. "Ah, actually, I was going to add a morning swim to my routine, then do my laps at night. That way my muscles won't be so stiff. I can help you put everything back after I finish my mile tonight."

"I didn't know swimming in the morning was an option," she said, surprised. "That sounds like a great way to start the day." She kissed him on the cheek.

Picking up Violet and her wicker stand, his mother carefully carried the plant into the kitchen out of harm's way.

Ryan stood under the shower for twenty minutes, letting the hot water beat the pain out of his aching head. He finished dressing as the painting crew rolled up. Grabbing his swim bag to make it look good, he was out the door before his mother could make any more great suggestions.

The morning swim thing had just been an excuse to dodge a breakfast he couldn't face, yet the more he thought about it, the more he liked the idea. A swim would do him good. It occurred to him that he had hit on a genius scheme. He could do his laps in the morning, which would leave all evening to play *Desert Death*. Slick and easy, it was the perfect plan, and no one would be the wiser. He adjusted his trajectory and wheeled toward the rec complex.

***

The water felt like mercury gliding across Ryan's skin. The early morning light streamed through the windows, making the pool sparkle. His head had stopped throbbing and his stomach settled as soon as he took his first stroke. It was as if swimming was some kind of miracle cure. Ryan felt better with each lap.

His arms burned from the exertion as he pulled powerfully, trying to shave off one, two, or three more seconds. Pull, breathe, pull — the rhythm sang in his ears, blocking all other sounds.

When he finally checked the clock, he couldn't believe it. It was his best time ever. He punched his fist in the air.

"Impressive! What's your name, son?"

Standing in the waist-deep water, Ryan whirled to see a man in a jogging suit with a whistle around his neck standing at the side of the pool.

Behind him, waiting on the deck, were the guys he had seen a couple of times during lane swimming, only now they had on swim caps with the logo *Sharks Swim Club* printed on the sides.

"What do you want to know for?"

"Because I have an interesting proposal, and calling you *son* seems rather impersonal."

The guy might be a nutcase, but he seemed harmless. "It's Ryan Taber."

The man dipped his head as though filing away the information. "I've seen you here before, Ryan. My name is Jim Kraus. I'm the coach, and I'd like to invite you to join the Sharks."

"Swim competitively? Me?" Ryan was unable to hide the shock in his voice. It would be a total jock thing to do, and that was unfamiliar territory for him.

The coach chuckled. "You might not be a medal contender this year. However, you have potential. Joining us is a good way to start. The Sharks plan on sweeping the championship, so you'll be part of a winning team."

Ryan had never considered competing before. The idea had its appeal. It would be a challenge, but the more he thought about it, the more right it felt. "Okay. You're on!"

"We do our training early in the morning. Do you think you can make it here three times a week?" the coach asked.

"Yeah, I can," Ryan grinned.

"See you tomorrow, six-thirty sharp!" Coach

Kraus nodded his approval. With a huge splash, Ryan's new teammates joined him in the pool, welcoming the newest Shark. Ryan had never felt so great. He could hardly wait to get home to e-mail old G.I.-*Drop-and-give-me-twenty* Jason.

Chapter 12

Things here are tense. Rocket attacks
nightly; suicide bombings more frequent. On
patrol, we watch every vehicle, every face,
every doorway. Fifteen million mines lie
silently waiting. Sappers mark the cleared
path through the minefield by painting boul-
ders — red on the dangerous side, white on
the safe — and you walk down the middle
between the coloured rocks. My buddy
working on a section of pathway behind a
village stepped on a hidden mine and both
of his legs disappeared.
It was supposed to be safe.
It was supposed to be safe.

Ryan reread the message. Gross and weird.
Jason's fingers must have stuttered and repeated
the last line. He imagined the dangerous work of

clearing a minefield. It would definitely be extreme.

Too bad about the guy getting blown up. Ryan had seen lots of casualties in *Desert Death*, some of them tragic. Still, the game went on. That was war.

And why nothing about the kick-ass Shark news? Maybe Jason hadn't received it before he sent the message.

Ryan checked his watch. That morning was to be his first official team swim, and he didn't want to be late, not after Coach's warning. He would write later when he had time to brag about his swimming coup in more detail. Ryan shut down the computer. It still felt great to be able to switch Jason off with the flick of a finger. He hurried downstairs feeling like a champion.

"Hi, honey," his mother greeted him. "The painters will be done today, so I'll need you to help me move everything back later." His mom was preparing to take the mutt for her morning constitutional and was searching for the leash. There were ladders, paint cans, and plastic sheeting everywhere, which made it a bit of a treasure hunt.

"Tonight? Sure," Ryan said absently as he stuffed a clean towel into his swim bag.

"It's a deal. I'll bring home a pizza and we can work on the furniture together. And this time," she gave him one of those mother-pulling-rank looks that bugged him so much, "no excuses, Ryan."

Grabbing his gear, he rushed out the door. His mother had morphed into some kind of Jekyll and Hyde. First, she was all teary and in need of cups of tea, then she lost her mind and deliberately did things they both knew Jason wouldn't go for, and now she was bossing Ryan around. It made Ryan's time with Casey even sweeter. No constant barrage of orders pounding him, and the only rules to follow were his own.

***

"Come on, faster, *faster!*" Coach yelled as he urged Ryan through the gruelling series of laps, each set using a different stroke.

Ryan pulled for all he was worth, trying to place his hands precisely to move as much water as possible. His form needed tweaking, and he remembered every word that Coach Kraus told him about fine-tuning his stroke. The coach had a way of making Ryan believe in himself, and he never raised his voice or made him feel like an idiot no matter what rookie mistake he made.

Ryan also listened to the advice that team captain Hugh McAllister offered on pacing, breathing, and clean turns.

When Ryan was sure he couldn't move his arms one more stroke, they finished the tough workout. Everyone gratefully hit the showers.

Hugh snapped his towel at Ryan as they dressed. "You did great. If I'm not careful, you'll end up giving me a run for the podium."

Ryan jumped out of the way and aimed a perfect retaliatory strike with his own towel. "Yeah, the coach hired me to keep you on your toes." Ryan liked the way everyone made him feel so accepted, especially Hugh. The team captain was one of the good ones.

As he left the rec complex, Ryan felt terrific and energized, ready to face whatever the day threw at him.

Chapter 13

School breezed by in a particularly satisfying way. Ryan even managed to enjoy Social Studies with Mr. Gregorwich, who really wasn't such a bad guy. At one point, Ryan stuck up his hand and answered a question correctly in front of the whole class. Mr. G. had been as surprised as Ryan.

Ryan's only disappointment had been that Chantal missed their one class together, which meant he didn't get to see her up close and personal. Despite deliberately passing by her locker a few times, Ryan still hadn't connected. He had decided he was going to ask her out to a movie for sure and, after the great morning he had had, there was finally something to talk about. He was now a Shark.

As Ryan loped down the stairs leaving school, he spotted Casey leaning against his car. The gamer had parked in a *Buses Only* zone, and the school buses would be arriving at any minute. It looked like trouble. Ryan was still ticked at the way Casey had treated him at the party, but walked over to warn him anyway.

"Dude, move your wheels or the Gestapo will be all over you. The buses will be here any second."

Casey seemed unconcerned as he pulled a package of cigarettes out of the pocket of his leather jacket. "I came to see if I could buy you a beer and a game of *D-Death* to make up for blowing you off. I was pretty lit and, well, you know how it goes." He held out the pack.

Ryan didn't smoke; no one in the Taber household would dream of engaging in that particular vice. Right at that moment, Ryan spotted Chantal leaving school. Her face glowed in the soft afternoon light, and Ryan stood a little taller when she waved and walked over.

"*Bonjour, mon ami*. I missed class today. I had an appointment at the *dentiste*." She laughed, a bright sparkling sound. "It was not so pleasant and I would have preferred to listen to Mr. G."

Chantal was looking particularly appealing wearing a tight-fitting lace top over her jeans, and Ryan noticed Casey checking her out. It made him want to show off.

He took the proffered smoke and lit it. "Hey, Chantal. Yeah, I wondered if you'd been hangin' last night and couldn't make it in. I nearly ditched for the same reason," he lied. The smoke burned

his lungs, and he hoped he wouldn't have a coughing fit.

Chantal looked taken aback, then confused.
"Hanging? Hanging what?"

Ryan tried to explain. "You know, too many
brewskies."

She still seemed lost and he gave up, resorting
to basics. "Beer! Lots and lots of beer!"

"Oh! I understand. No, I had only the *dentiste*."

Mr. Gregorwich picked that moment to push
through the crowd and stand in front of them.

"The buses are coming and you'll have to move
this car." He stopped when he saw the cigarette.
"Ryan, you know smoking is not allowed on
school property."

Ryan wasn't about to wimp out now, not in front
of Chantal. He took a long drag on his cigarette
and fought the urge to gag. "Don't get excited, Mr.
G. It's just a smoke, and class is out, right?"

Colour suffused the teacher's face. "I don't
know what's gotten into you. Either put that thing
out or get off school property, *now*!"

Casey snorted and Ryan knew he was eating
this up. Ryan felt like a rebel. He felt powerful.
"Don't have a stroke. It's just a butt."

"Ryan, you're looking at a suspension. Now,
put that out."

Ryan took a long drag on the cigarette, slowly
exhaling the smoke in an odorous blue cloud.

"That's it, Mr. Taber. You've just pulled a one-
day suspension."

Ryan almost choked. Suspended! He had never been in trouble at school in his life. The bottom dropped out of his stomach. But then he saw Chantal's eyes grow round with what he was sure must be awe. A day's suspension was a cheap price for that look. He straightened. "Come on, Casey. You said you'd buy me a beer."

Ryan flicked his cigarette onto the ground at his teacher's feet and climbed into the car. Mr. Gregorwich went purple with rage. The last thing Ryan saw as they sped out of the parking lot was Chantal's face. Her expression seemed to have gone from awe to shock. He had a small shiver of doubt: perhaps he had gone too far.

"Hey, when did you grow a set?" Casey asked as he cut in and out of traffic.

"What?" Ryan refocused. "Oh, Gregorwich is such a suit. He lives for the stupid school rules, like the whole place would come crashing down if anyone had an independent thought." Guilt flashed, making him feel lousy. He liked Mr. G., and now he was trashing him.

"That's why I ditched high school. It was a waste of my talents, and it sounds like it's a waste of yours."

Ryan heard something new in Casey's voice: respect. Okay, maybe he'd been over the top with Mr. G. But that look on Chantal's face, and respect from HacknSlash … man, that made it all worthwhile. How he was going to explain a suspension to his mother was the tricky part — especially for smoking. He would cross that bridge when he came to it. He was the Warrior Monk, a Terminator. He was the real deal.

Ryan and Casey stayed at the café for a long time. The level of the game was at an all-time high. Ryan was on fire. He knew he had missed his supper, but so what? His mother would have to deal. Something fuzzy in the back of his mind nagged at him … Then it hit him. He had forgotten the whole paint-the-living-room-move-the-furniture-back thing. His hand touched the cell phone in his pocket. She had called earlier, but when he had seen *Mom* on the call display, he hadn't answered. Phoning now would be a disaster.

He needed to fix this if he could. He would do it in the morning, before he left for school. Then he remembered. He didn't have to go to school the next day — he was suspended. And after that, it was the weekend. A three-day weekend, not too shabby. Right now, all Ryan cared about was that he was playing better than he ever had, and he wasn't about to cut it short.

HacknSlash had taught him well, and Ryan attacked the game with a ruthlessness he didn't know he possessed. He tortured, maimed, and killed without a second thought. His *Ethical Rating* had bottomed out; his scores, however, were through the roof. He was a Terminator and the ground shook when he walked. His life had turned into an R-rated movie since he'd met Casey. He and Casey had had some wicked adventures in the short time they had known each other. Ryan remembered the wild ride through the city, the guys in the black SUV in hot pursuit. Everything was always so extreme with the guy — his skill at gaming, the late-night parties and the way he blasted through the city. That reminded him:

"Hey, man, way back, those goons in the black Escalade, did you get that straightened out? They totally meant business." Ryan fired his rocket launcher, blowing up another villager's house. Rats! Two more civilian kills. No biggie.

"I got rid of them. Nothing to it." Casey said, taking out three Nomads with a cleverly placed chunk of C-4.

Ryan caught a quick shot of HacknSlash's screen, and it made his stomach twist. He was doing a victory dance over the freshly dead.

Casey continued talking. "Just in case, I'm laying low. The Hag would go off the rails if anything happened to her precious car while I'm driving it."

The tidbit of info surprised Ryan. "That's your mother's car?"

Casey looked at him like he was the lowest noob in the game. "You think I have the cash to buy a sled like that? Hardly. She lets me borrow it to do errands for her."

"Oh, right." Ryan frowned. Casey's revelation that he didn't own the car shouldn't really matter, and yet, somehow, it did.

When he got home, Ryan looked into the living room as he passed through to the kitchen. He stared at the previously shabby room. Not only was the painting finished, his mother had managed to rearrange the furniture without his help.

And it was their old furniture that held his attention. It now sported striped green and beige covers, which made the old junk look new. Had some rich aunt died and left them a small fortune? Was the world coming to an end on Tuesday, and had his mom decided to spend his inheritance early?

Ryan breezed into the kitchen, hoping his mom wouldn't give him too much grief. He decided the strong approach was best. "Hey, where'd those sheet things on the furniture come from? They look expensive — maybe you should have waited till Christmas." He grabbed a hunk of cheese and a slice of bread. He'd had a burrito at the café, easy one-handed food that didn't interfere with his game controller, but it hadn't been enough.

His mother turned and looked at him coolly. "They're called slipcovers, and I put them on when I moved all the furniture back *by myself*. Right now we have another matter to discuss. Sit down."

Her voice was unnaturally calm. But Ryan could hear a dangerous undertone, like the rumble of a volcano. He sat, his stomach sinking. He had been busted for sure, and knew the volcano was about to erupt.

"Principal Finn called …"

He looked at the floor. *There she blows*!

"She said you've been suspended for smoking!

For crying out loud, Ryan, *suspended*! I can't believe it. *Sus-pend-ed!*" She said the word slowly, emphasizing every syllable. "And for smoking! This is completely unacceptable on all counts. When your father hears this, he's going to be devastated. *Smoking*, for God's sake!"

"Yeah, well, I'm giving it up." He mumbled.

"*Giving it up!*" The calm was gone. "Too bad you didn't give it up yesterday, then you wouldn't be suspended today! I spent an hour in Principal Finn's office talking about this situation. This is so unlike you, Ryan. We're both very worried." She held up her hand as if to stop the disaster, then looked at her watch. "It's zero-eight-hundred in Afghanistan. Your father's call is due to come through. I'll talk to him and then Principal Finn, and we'll decide what you should do to make this right."

Ryan stomped upstairs, the smell of fresh paint following him like a guilty conscience.

***

When his mom came into his room, Ryan knew he was in for the old heart-to-heart. It looked like she had been crying, but he forgot about that the second she started in with the lecture. His parents had come up with what they thought was a suitable punishment. Jason probably loved mulling that one over long and hard, like pulling the wings off a fly.

"Your dad and I discussed it, and have decided you will apologize to Mr. Gregorwich and also to Principal Finn. Plus you will make a *Stop Smoking* poster for the school cafeteria. As this is your first problem at school and these are special circumstances, with your father away, we're giving you the benefit of the doubt and hope that you'll clean up your act. You'll be grounded over the weekend and, since there's no smoking in this house, it will help your efforts to quit cold turkey. Oh, and Ryan, your father doesn't want to talk about this again. It's too disappointing. Understood?"

Ryan almost burst out laughing. A poster! As if! If he had known getting out of trouble would be so easy, he would have gotten into some way earlier. He went to bed that night feeling like he had turned a page in the book of his extreme new life.

Chapter 14

Soldier. Bad things all around. Kids carrying IEDs, suicide grandmothers — you never know. We've been in several firefights. Weapons come in all shapes and sizes, from sticks and stones to missiles. I've been assigned to guard the new outer perimeter line. The distance to the wire isn't much, still it grows farther every day. Sometimes when I'm on guard duty, it's like I can see the safe zone sliding away, leaving me behind.

The message ended there. Ryan could hardly believe it. True to his word, Jason was saving the lecture until he got home and could really dial it up, which was okay with Ryan. His mother had made him spend his suspension day doing chores around the house — which sucked, as he had planned on going to CyberKnights the second she left for work. Then he and his mom had spent some "quality time" together on the weekend, which had turned out to be a total bust. She kept trying to get him to talk about things, as though she could understand anything in his world.

Something else was kind of weird — Jason still hadn't said anything about Ryan becoming a member of the Sharks, other than to remind him not to forget his laps. It was as if Jason hadn't received Ryan's e-mail at all. Or he had decided to disregard it, which was more likely.

Monday morning, Ryan prepared to get the apologies over with before anyone at school, like Chantal, saw him. He arrived early and quickly finished with Principal Finn, who gave him a gentle lecture. Then he went to Mr. G.'s classroom.

He gave the door a quick knock and walked in. The second he saw the hard look on his favourite teacher's face, his confidence faltered. He had thought this would be no sweat, but found that the words stuck. Ryan cleared his throat, reminding himself that he was the one in control here. "Last week, ah, I … About the smoking thing …" He made his voice sound convincingly contrite. "I came to apologize."

Mr. Gregorwich tossed his pen onto his desk. "Okay, I'm listening."

"Actually, Mr. G., I don't know what came over me. It was a serious mistake and I'm really sorry. I thought about it all weekend and I've learned my lesson." Ryan figured this was enough garbage to satisfy any teacher.

Mr. Gregorwich waited a second, then leaned his chair back on two legs and laced his hands behind his head. "I bet you didn't know this about me, Ryan, but I grew up on a farm near a little town called Tomahawk, here in Alberta. We raised dairy cows and a few head of horses. So you see," his teacher continued, "I've had more experience shovelling manure than you ever will, so don't try heaping this crap on me! You should have been suspended for a month, not a day!" He dropped his chair to the floor with a bang. "You were out-and-out disrespectful, not just to me — to your fellow students and to this school. The staff and student body here have a good working relationship, and we are all trying to make your lives success stories. As far as I'm concerned, with an attitude like the one you demonstrated, your chance of being one of those success stories has been seriously damaged." He straightened some papers on his desk, signalling that their meeting was over.

Speechless, Ryan turned to leave.

"And, Ryan, have the *Stop Smoking* poster up by the end of the day."

Ryan swallowed. He hadn't expected any of this, and he sure hadn't planned on actually making the ridiculous poster. Anger flooded him. Who did this chalk-chewer think he was? Ryan left cursing under his breath.

By now, the school was filling with students. Ryan noticed the strange looks they were giving him in the hallways. Perhaps the news — or better, the *fame* — of what he had done had spread. It was a little odd that everyone seemed to avoid him. Maybe they didn't know what to say to a tough guy like him? This made him feel in control again and he took on a confident air as he strutted to his locker. It sucked that his first class was back with Mr. G., but Ryan was glad that by having their meeting early he had avoided playing out that scene in front of his classmates, especially Chantal.

Ryan made sure he was the last student to enter the classroom, noting the murmur that followed him as he strode to his desk.

Chantal, in a pale pink shirt with three buttons undone, looked extremely hot, especially when she bent over to take a binder out of her pack. After showing her that he wouldn't be pushed around, Ryan was ready to move forward. He had never asked a girl out before and Chantal Roy was definitely the way to start. Maybe he would take her to one of Casey's wild parties and show her he was no longer the wimpy guy she had first met weeks ago.

He didn't have the opportunity during class, but Warrior Monk was ready the second the dismissal bell rang.

"Hey, Chantal, you want to have lunch with me today?" Ryan asked. "I've got lots to tell you."

"I will work on my banner project at lunch."

Chantal picked up her pack and started down the aisle.

Ryan hadn't factored this response into his battle scenario. "This banner, are you doing it in the art room? I could meet you there. I kind of have a little project myself." He thought of the dumb poster. Working on it with Chantal by his side would make it a reward.

She didn't turn around.

"Catch you later!" he called as she left. He guessed her banner would involve more *Go Canada Go* cheerleading like *Support Our Troops* or *We're Behind You All the Way!* Ryan had seen that stuff all over the base, and hoped the sentiment meant the fighting would continue for a long time. It crossed his mind that, when he was old enough to enlist, he might be sent to Afghanistan to carry on the fight. Conflicts like that one were open-ended. They kept going forever with no real resolution, and fresh violence would erupt whenever some new faction or army marched in and tried to fix things. Look how long the fighting in the Gaza Strip and Bosnia had lasted. After all his practice with *Desert Death*, Ryan felt it would be awesome to be there in person.

At lunch, he went to the art room, but Chantal wasn't there. Maybe she hadn't heard him when he said he would meet her here. Surely she wouldn't want to miss out on a chance to be with him, not after the look she'd given him when he was punking Mr. G.? Rummaging in the paper cupboard,

Ryan found a large sheet of bristol board and a few felt markers. No one said it had to be art. He wrote the first line: *Got a Nasty Habit?* This was followed by the words *WHY not STOP NOW!* He made the "why," "stop," and "now" in large, heavy black capital letters, and wrote the word "not" very small in pale yellow marker. He drew a picture of a rolled item that looked more like a huge marijuana joint than a commercial cigarette. When he stood back to admire his work, he grunted with satisfaction. At a distance, the word *not* disappeared leaving the message to read: *Got a Nasty Habit? WHY STOP NOW?* with the suspicious-looking cigarette smouldering underneath. Perfect! He reached into his jacket pocket and took out the last detail to give his poster the impact it needed.

Marching into the noisy cafeteria, he proudly hung his masterpiece for all to admire. As he finished tacking the last corner up, the sudden silence told him he had every kid's attention.

He had made a pile of fake joints and glued them around his rendering of the fat reefer. Pleased with the effect, Ryan crisply saluted his work of art.

It was right then that Ms. Johnson and Mr. Rath, his two least-favourite math teachers, walked through the doors. Ballistic would probably be a good word to describe their reactions.

The snickering started as they hauled him out of the room.

Chapter 15

Ryan spent the afternoon in the detention room next to the admin office, and there was a family conference scheduled for after school. This time he was invited to the meeting. As he sat waiting for his mother to arrive, he felt great. They couldn't bust him; it was their idea for him to make a poster with an anti-smoking theme. And he couldn't very well have used real cigarettes; he didn't have any and wasn't old enough to buy his own. Was it his fault he was a poor artist and the replicas resembled something other than commercial cancer sticks?

By the time his mother arrived, Ryan knew every crack and scar in the ugly beige walls. He had decided he hated the colour, if beige was even a real colour. His mom walked into the room and stood in front of him. She didn't yell or rant, only looked at him for an uncomfortably long time. It was the expression on her face that hit him hard. It was a look of such total disappointment that he would have way rather she had yelled.

"I don't know what to say, Ryan. I'm so sorry I've let you down."

If he had been standing, he would have fallen over. This was the last thing he expected her to say. As they went into the principal's office, he felt like hell.

"I don't understand what went wrong, Principal Finn," his mother began. "I thought Ryan understood that we were giving him a chance to redeem himself. Unfortunately, he seems to have used this as an opportunity to do the opposite. He's having a few problems and needs to work on things." She put her hand on his arm. "At his age, he is pretty much responsible for himself. All I can do is continue to love and support him. The rest is up to my son."

Her voice quavered the tiniest bit. Ryan couldn't look at his mother. Instead, he suddenly found a hangnail on his thumb very interesting.

Principal Finn laced her fingers together and sighed. "Ryan, can you explain why you made your poster so confrontational? You had to know you'd get in trouble."

The principal's voice was very calm, which threw Ryan a little off balance. He had expected fireworks. Ryan started to give them the speech about his lack of artistic talent, then trailed off lamely. "... I guess I'm no artist, and didn't realize the fake cigarettes could be mistaken for marijuana."

Principal Finn shook her head.

"I feel this approach is not working; and I don't think suspending you again will improve things. At best, you used poor judgment and poorer taste; at worst, you deliberately tried to get yourself kicked out of school, and I can't believe you would do that, Ryan. You can take your poster home; we don't want it here. And if it's attention you want, you won't be getting any of that either — no more posters, no public apology to the student body or the teachers. This matter will be closed. You can consider this strike two, young man. And believe me, *three strikes and you're out.* Do you understand, Ryan?" She made a note in his file, underscoring several words in strong strokes of black ink before continuing.

"I know our families are under a lot of pressure, especially those with loved ones in Afghanistan. This must be very hard on your mom, Ryan, and I hope you keep that in mind the next time you have to make a decision that could land you in my office."

His mother was silent as they left the school. Ryan didn't know what to say either. Instead, he kicked feebly at a stone, sending it spinning along the sidewalk. Then, his mother did a remarkable thing. She walked over to a small blue Honda Civic in the visitor's parking lot and stuck a key in the lock!

Ryan stared, confused. "What are you doing?"

"I'm getting into our car so we can go home."

"*Our* car?" Ryan had moved past confused and was now astonished. "You're telling me you bought a car?"

"As a matter of fact, I did. One of the vet's clients bought a new Lexus and wanted to sell this little gem. The money from my job made it possible."

He knew she had always wanted a car. He had heard his parents arguing over it many times, with Jason always winning. That was the point: Jason won on the *no car* thing every time, and now this? It was too much. Ryan didn't think he could keep up with his mother and her surprises. He wondered — if Jason stayed away long enough, maybe he could get that Ducati motorcycle he lusted after.

His mother went on. "I was worried about being away from home so much and, from this afternoon's incident, I'd say I had good cause. The car will save me a couple of hours a day on the bus. It makes sense."

They climbed in and his mother started the engine. Ryan loved the car the instant he heard the motor purr to life. He would have to get his learner's permit right away. He could already imagine himself behind the wheel, cruising with Chantal beside him, her hand on his thigh …

His mother broke in on his pleasant thoughts. "I couldn't believe it when Principal Finn called. My

God, Ryan, staying out late, drinking, …"

Ryan's head came up in surprise. How had she known?

"a school suspension. And now, when you had a chance to make things right, you pull this foolish stunt with the poster. What do you expect us to do? I thought you were growing up, and I gave you a lot of slack when your dad left. I think I made a mistake. The behaviour you've shown is anything but grown-up."

Ryan studiously looked out the car window. He knew his mother was ramping up for an all-out attack and that he had better defuse the situation in a hurry. With a little finesse, he should be able to get himself out of this. He turned to her. "I made a mistake, took things too far. It won't happen again, Mom."

He had put what he hoped was the perfect note of apology in his voice and saw her death grip on the wheel relax.

"It's not that simple, Ryan. I'll talk to your father and we'll take it from there. Oh, and I don't want you to tell your dad about the car," she added.

He looked at her suspiciously. "So I'm part of yet another homegrown conspiracy?"

"Not at all." She raised her chin defiantly. "It's a great surprise, and since I'm the one who made it happen, you can forget about spoiling my fun. I know your dad will be thrilled."

"I'm not sure *thrilled* is the right word."

"Nonsense. He'll love the car and, once he gets used to it, he'll enjoy the convenience of owning our own transportation and not having to rely on the bus or friends every time we want to go somewhere."

"You don't have to convince me, Mom. I'm pumped." Considering how his day had gone, this was a great way to wind it up. He had managed to cause a sensation at school, get a pass from the principal, and turn a bad situation around with his mother.

Yeah, he was smarter than God.

Chapter 16

Later that night, Ryan was playing on his computer when his mom eased the door to his room open. "Honey, I spoke to your father and we need to talk."

He could tell from the look on her face that he was about to get slammed.

She sat in a chair opposite him, looking tired. "Needless to say, your dad was very disappointed."

The idea of going over this afternoon's little problem again made him want to scream. Why did she have to tattle to General Jase? He thought they had things settled. Unexpectedly, his temper spiked.

"For crying out loud, Mom, I said I was sorry. You didn't have to turn it into a federal case."

His mother was instantly on her feet. "That's enough attitude. You are the one who messed up,

Ryan, not me. We've decided that, in addition to your grounding, which will continue until further notice, you will fill any spare time by doing odd jobs for other families on the base who have spouses in Afghanistan. I'll make a list of jobs you can do, starting with cleaning your room. It smells like a gorilla cage in there. Then you can mow our lawn and anyone else's in the neighbourhood who wants theirs done. You need to take responsibility for those decisions you've been making. Your father says he'll talk to you about this when he gets home. For now, the matter is closed." She left his room, shutting the door a little harder than she had to.

Ryan was so pissed that he could have punched something. The grounding thing sucked. He could still swim though, and thanks to his genius, he had already set things up to allow him some *Desert Death* time. Maybe he could figure a way to "swim" even more times a week. The one thing that G.I. Jason hadn't counted on was that the Warrior Monk could endure any kind of torture.

***

Soldier. Bad things are happening daily. Can't sleep. The noise in my head never stops, even when the guns are silent. It's not like I thought over here. Take care of your mother; be sure to take care of your mother.

Jason's e-mails were getting shorter and stranger. He was either very busy or had decided to blow off his long-winded chats. Ryan was disappointed. The first e-mails from his father had mostly been boring with all the save-the-world stuff, then they had switched and been about the closely pitched battles, the fear of roadside bombs and snipers, and the rising death toll. The details had been fierce.

Now, his father's e-mails had changed again to this weird stuff, and Ryan wondered why old Jason was holding out on the juicy goods. It made him glad he had saved the earlier ones. He reread them, reliving the battles and dangerous patrols. The scenes came to life in his mind: he was the one deploying the troops, using brilliant strategy to lead the men to victory. He smashed the enemy with his superior tactics in the firefights. Wicked!

Ryan hit *delete*.

***

To ensure his mother couldn't issue any more orders, Ryan set his alarm and left earlier than usual to swim with the Sharks. Mom was turning into a pretty darn good facsimile of old Jase, and Ryan didn't like it.

He swam harder and faster than he ever had, and Coach Kraus congratulated him in front of his teammates after practice.

"I know, with the way the team is shaping up,

we're going to bring home gold. Each and every one of you is out-performing all my expectations, especially our newest Shark, Ryan Taber. Son, you were born to swim! Great work. You keep this up and I might put you in the relay at the Provincials."

Hugh had spent a lot of extra time doing laps with Ryan and helping with his technique. Grinning mischievously, he hip-checked Ryan, sending him back into the pool they had just climbed out of.

Ryan should have seen it coming. Bumping unsuspecting teammates into the water was a time-honoured tradition among the Sharks, and made him feel like he was truly part of the team.

He sputtered to the surface, laughing, and then splashed his buddy before taking Hugh's offered hand. It felt good to bask in the praise and Ryan also felt that it was justified. He had worked hard for this.

Chapter 17

Practically oozing confidence, Ryan could hardly wait to see Chantal and ask her on the long-anticipated date. Today was the day. He would ditch a night of *Desert Death* and take Chantal to a movie instead. His mother would be no wiser and, with the money he had made mowing all those stupid lawns, he could afford it.

He chuckled to himself at how well the lawn fiasco had turned out. Offering to cut the neighbours' lawns for free was genius, especially when he added the part about how it took his mind off worrying about dear old daddy fighting near Kandahar. Man, the wallets opened up then, and he ended up with nearly fifty bucks for a couple of hours' work. His mother couldn't very well complain if he got tipped for a job well done.

By the time he reached school, Ryan was so excited, he felt on fire. He muscled past the annoying students in the hallway, leaving a trail of nasty comments in his wake. He had spiked his hair, which had finally grown enough to comb, and made sure his breath was fresh. He saw Chantal setting up a table with a poster display in the Speaker's Corner, where students were allowed to vent about whatever subject they wanted for one week. Usually it was about legalizing soft drugs or putting condom machines in the washrooms. It was as if the gods were smiling on him. Straightening, he walked over.

"Hey, Chantal, more war gore?" He winced. That was a totally lame opening.

She barely noticed him. "Oh, hi, Ryan."

Okay, this was not how it was supposed to go. She was supposed to say, *Bonjour, Ryan, how thrilling to see you. Nothing is new with me, what is new with you, mon amour?* That would give him the opportunity to tell her about his upcoming swimming competition. She would be so impressed, she'd be hounding *him* for a date!

"I have no time now. I have to unveil my banner." Her tone was distracted as she continued to unpack the box on the table.

"Unveil ..."

"Pardon?" she asked with a frown.

"I could help you unveil, *put up*, the banner."

The look she gave him came as a surprise. From anyone else, he would say it was on the frosty side.

"I can do it. I need only the thumbnails." She

reached for a yogurt container and opened the lid.

He laughed when he saw what was inside. "Thumb*tacks*! So what's the banner in aid of? Orphaned puppies, save-the-children, the homeless?" he teased.

She turned her huge blue eyes on him and he saw steel in them. "*Non.*" She fixed one end of the banner to the wall behind the table and then moved to secure the other end.

Ryan watched her bustling about, thinking she was the cutest girl in the school, and how he desperately wanted to go out with her. He took a deep breath. It was now or never, and he wanted her *now*. "So, I was wondering, if you're not busy Saturday night, maybe you and I could …"

She unfolded the bright green strip of material and Ryan was stunned into silence. It read *BRING OUR TROOPS HOME! CANADA OUT OF AFGHANISTAN NOW!*

"It is to protest our troops in Afghanistan," Chantal explained. "I took photos of our basketball and soccer teams, student clubs and activities. I went to the park and took more photos of mothers with their children, kids doing skateboarding, and dogs playing, everything I could think of to show what our soldiers are risking and what they left at home. All these are printed on the banner."

Ryan was speechless. *Bring our troops home?* He thought of his father hammering through the desert in his LAV, blasting the low-lifes. That was an experience anyone would think was fantastic. Besides, he liked Jason gone. Life was way better with his father thousands of kilometres away — they had a car, a nicer house. Ryan even had a cell phone!

And Ryan liked his freedom. Why would he want Jason home? The Tabers would have to go back to life the way it had been — and that was not an option.

Chantal turned to him. "Will you sign my petition?"

He couldn't believe it. "Are you kidding? In case you haven't figured this part out, we live on a military base; this is a school on that base. How did you get permission to put that up?"

"Also, we live in a democracy. The principal, she said she may not agree with my opinion, but she respects my right to express it in an open forum — on the student bulletin boards, anyway."

"Chantal, I like my father being gone. He can spend the next ten years over there for all I care." Ryan's feelings boiled to the surface. "And I'm sick of hearing all this garbage about bringing the troops home. *They're soldiers* — that's what they do! If they were here, they'd march around a parade square and go on fake manoeuvres. Over there, they can shoot at a real enemy and use real bullets. Let the boys do their job."

Now it was her turn to look surprised. "I don't agree with that at all, Ryan." She shook her head, causing her hair to swirl around her head like a bronze halo. "No war is worth the life of one single child, no matter if that child is six and playing on a Kabul street or twenty-six and wearing a Canadian uniform."

Finished with hanging the banner, she returned the yogurt container to the box and put it under the table. "Why can't two countries, *two peoples*, exist without one trying to shoot the other in the head because they think in different ways? Our government has decided to make the whole planet in their image. Their armies are forcing the Afghan people to defend democracy, when they do not even know what it is. *Merde!* If the people don't want freedom enough to fight for it themselves, what will happen when our troops leave? If it returns to the way it was, then all our soldiers, *all those children*, will be dead for nothing."

She had launched into speech mode, and Ryan had no idea how to stop her. A crowd had gathered, listening as she voiced her opinion.

"The way we live is right for us because it is what we know. Don't you understand, Ryan? The opposite works for them because it's what they know, what they always have known. Of what right do we march in and tell them the system they spent centuries developing is wrong because it doesn't conform to our model? What is it that makes our way more right than their way?"

Her voice was passionate and the speech compelling. Ryan had never seen her like this before. Gone was the quiet French–Canadian girl of his dreams, and in her place was Joan of freaking Arc!

He didn't know what to say as she stormed on.

"Ryan, this is turning into the new Crusades, no? It is our prophet against their prophet, Jesus versus Muhammad! It is the Christian world against the Islamic world all over again. Extremists? No, but what if they are only trying to protect a way of life — *their* way of life?"

He had heard enough. What was wrong with her? Didn't she understand the big picture? "Their *way of life*? If roadside bombs are their *way of life*, then they need it changed. Don't kid yourself, Chantal! Our troops are fighting so that people in Afghanistan can at least have a shot at picking the way they want to live. If you don't know what options are out there, how can you make a choice?"

"One does not choose freely while standing at the barrel of a gun," she said defiantly.

He shook his head. "You bleeding hearts are all the same. This is not a polite war with everyone following the rules of engagement. There's a price to pay for freedom. Someone has to draw a line in the sand, and Canada is making sure the right hand holds the stick."

"We *bleeding hearts* want to make sure that the price isn't too high on either side," she spit back.

Her jaw clenched very much like Jason's did when he was spouting his own rhetoric, and that one gesture added fuel to Ryan's fire. His temper exploded. "This is the twenty-first century, Chantal, and it's time everyone lived in the here and now, not back in the dark ages. The only way to end this is to finish the Taliban and Al-Qaida once and for all. Stop pussyfooting around, and send in a nuclear strike to melt every damn one of them into the sand."

The shocked look on her face shut him up. It was obvious she was appalled at his simple solution. It had worked at Hiroshima and Nagasaki in 1945. The war was decisively over within days of the nukes being dropped. Why not Afghanistan, where war had raged for centuries? Start again with a clean slate.

Chantal took an involuntary step backward, her face stricken. "That is truly disgusting." Her eyes looked wet and her voice dropped to little more than a whisper. "When we met, I liked you, Ryan. Then I saw how you treated other students and how you cut class. I thought it was just male bravado, showing off, and that you would straighten out. But the way you behave, with the smoking and the disrespect to Mr. Gregorwich, I became worried that maybe you have issues too big for me to deal with. Your Afghan *final solution* makes me see that we have nothing in common." Turning to the crowd, she held up her petition. "I am here to ask for your signatures to send to Ottawa, with the hope that our leaders will listen to the voice of reason and bring our troops home before the war escalates," she glanced at Ryan. "And people melt into the sand."

Ryan walked away. This was not how the

whole scene was supposed to play out. Free speech? It was like she had a double standard: it was fine for her to say ridiculous things like "Stop the war," but when he said what he thought, he was a monster.

Chapter 18

Casey had asked Ryan to do another pickup, and since Ryan's mother had a late shift, he wouldn't have to worry about a lecture if he was a little delayed getting home. He rode to the battered old house, and the grungy biker handed him the small package, exactly like the half-dozen times Ryan had done HacknSlash the same favour.

He stuffed the box into his jacket and was about to get on his bicycle, when a hand on his shoulder made him freeze. The iron grip was excruciating. Ryan dropped to his knees.

"You're going to take Ardmore a message for us." The voice was like gravel.

Ryan looked up into the mirrored sunglasses and acne-scarred face of Goon Number One from the SUV. Goon Two hung back, checking out the neighbourhood. Ryan thought he was probably watching for witnesses.

"Yeah, what?" Ryan croaked.

The hulk leaned down close to Ryan's ear. He smelled of a subtle and probably expensive after-shave, instead of the rancid garlic hitmen always stank of in gangster movies. "Tell him he owes us ten big ones, and the meter's running."

Ryan winced. These thugs were exactly why God invented Uzis.

No way was he going to show them how scared he was. He staggered to his feet, shaking off the guy's hairy paw. "Why don't you tell him your-self?"

"We tried. It seems he isn't getting the mes-sage. Are *you* getting the message, *Ryan*?"

The use of his name surprised him. How much did these low-lifes know about him?

"Maybe your mother, who works *alone* late at night at that flea-bag animal hospital, would understand better than you. You sure you want to be a runner for Ardmore, kid? He's the kind of boss who'd throw you to the lions to save his own hide."

The two leg-breakers retreated and left Ryan shaking and sweating. He took several deep calm-ing breaths and tried to think of what he should do next.

***

Ryan held the box up to the closed-circuit camera as he banged on the door. "Open up! It's me!"

The door opened and Ryan burst in. "Do you want to tell me why those two guys hassled me tonight? They said you owed them ten thousand dollars! Casey, what the hell is going on?"

Casey took the package and tossed it on the chair. "Idiots! I told them I'd get them some cash by next week. Did they try to squeeze you for money? They must be dumber than I thought, 'cause it's obvious you don't have two toonies to rub together."

"Casey, they threatened me and my mom. Like, if you don't pay, we get to pay — with our skins."

"Take it easy. Those two are all talk. They're not going to do anything, trust me." Casey laughed and turned away. "Want a beer?"

Ryan grabbed his arm and spun him around. "What's this about? What are you into?"

Facing him now, Casey replied, "I told you. These guys are trying to shake me down, and I refuse to play along. Their problem is they won't take no for an answer, and I won't give in. A guy's got to take a stand, right?"

He sounded so sincere, Ryan faltered, then dropped his friend's arm. "Are you being straight with me?"

"Trust me, I'll take care of you. I'm the golden goose, so those enforcers won't touch me. And you … you have nothing to do with the business. You're merely an innocent bystander."

Ryan had never had a friend like Casey. He figured that, after all their adventures, he should give him the benefit of the doubt. Then he remembered the threat to his mother. "Even innocent bystanders can end up as collateral damage."

***

Ryan was watching TV when his mother and the dog came home. They didn't have cable, another unneeded luxury, which meant he was stuck with peasant vision and endless reruns of *The Simpsons*. She tossed her backpack down and, without acknowledging him, walked directly over to the little houseplant sitting in the wicker stand.

"Hi, and how was your day, Ruff Cut?" Ryan said, his tone skirting flippant. The mangy dog wagged her tail hopefully at the unexpected attention.

His mom examined the plant, which was looking very healthy and green. "It's odd. I've practically been ignoring this little thing, and it's thriving. I guess sometimes you have to stop fussing so things can develop on their own, the way they should. I thought I was helping; it seems I was interfering. Violet has done nicely all by herself."

Carefully, she peeked under a leaf, and then clapped her hands like an excited child. "Yes! Flowers! And they're pink! I love pink flowers!"

She gave the plant a wide smile, then turned to Ryan. "I feel like pizza. You up for some frozen pizza?"

Ryan watched her. In the fading light streaming

through their living-room window, she looked different, more like the modern business women he saw in office buildings, the type who were smart and ended up on the cover of some ladies' magazine. He had never seen his mother that way before.

The TV program was interrupted by an urgent report of three soldiers injured in a suicide bombing in Kandahar. His mother immediately went rigid.

In an instant, she turned into the tired, anxious mother he remembered, as if all the light in her had been extinguished. Her brow creased as she focused on the small screen, her attention riveted. When the announcer said it had been three British troops, she exhaled. Her hand shook as she smoothed back her short hair. "I'll … get … ah, the pizza, yes, I'll go put the pizza in the oven."

She left the room and Ryan waited, then he heard her exclamation of delight.

Thanks to the disaster with Chantal, Ryan still had the cash he had saved to take her out. So he had stopped at the grocery store and picked up some kind of leafy plant to keep his mom's scraggly violet company. The lady said it was bulletproof and that anyone could keep it alive. He knew it would make his mom happy, and he felt good being able to give her a present. Besides, it might score him a few points, which couldn't hurt.

She walked back into the living room holding the small potted vine. "This is wonderful, Ryan.

I've always wanted a Pothos. Thank you so much!"

Her eyes were shining and she had reverted to the younger version of herself, the one who didn't scan TV screens for war sound bites or study the paper for casualty statistics. He liked this mom. "No problem," he said, feeling a little embarrassed at her excitement over something so trivial.

That night, his mind wouldn't shut up. The harder he tried, the more sleep was out of the question. He had so much swirling in his head that he thought it would explode. He was worried about his mom and, although Casey told him not to take it seriously, the goon's threat had shaken him. Casey said he had paid what he owed, yet they were pressuring him for a whole lot more. He knew HacknSlash was a tough guy and didn't want to give in, but they weren't going to take no for an answer. It was a grim situation. Still, there was no way Ryan was going to quit on his friend.

Then there was Chantal, his sweet Chantal. All that garbage about bringing the troops home and stopping the war was simply unpatriotic crazy talk. He was sure that the blow-up had been some weird aberration, and the right thing to do would be to give her another chance.

Yeah, he'd give her another chance.

Ryan relaxed and drifted off.

Chapter 19

The next day, Ryan's life detonated.

Ryan had let his schoolwork slip a little. Okay, a lot. His teachers, especially Mr. G., were hounding him for overdue reports and missed assignments, threatening to make his life a living hell if he didn't produce. And sure enough, things had gotten hot. It was like they had convened a secret meeting in the staff room and decided it was *Get Ryan Taber Day*.

He made up excuses and promised the undeliverable to keep out of the principal's office. Maybe his new style could use a little tweaking; never knowing when he would walk into an ambush was getting old. After one of the worst days he could remember, he was actually looking forward to heading home and escaping to the solitude of his room.

When he dragged himself in from school, Ryan

found his mother sitting in her favourite chair. One look at her face and he froze; dread immediately swallowed him whole.

He scanned the tidy room, looking for any signs that a Notification Party had been here. They were the military messengers that informed next of kin when a loved one had been killed in action.

He could see nothing out of the ordinary. His mother always kept the living room immaculate, just in case. She didn't want the base gossips to say her house was a mess when she heard.

"Mom," he said quietly, "is everything okay?" She looked at him with tear-swollen eyes and he feared the worst. "Is it Jason?"

"Yes …"

Ryan felt like he had been punched in the gut.

His assumption must have registered on his face, because she hurried on. "No, no, it's not what you think. Ryan, your father's coming home! I got a call this afternoon saying Jason was on a troop transport in Dubai and would be here soon. Isn't that wonderful?"

Ryan stared at her in disbelief. "His rotation isn't up yet. Why is he coming home?"

His mother looked down at her scruffy dog as it nudged her leg for a pat. "It's why we haven't heard from him in so long. He's been sick, and the medical officer I spoke to said he needed some R-and-R." The corners of her mouth curved up weakly. "You know, a little homegrown peace and quiet with us."

Rest and recreation at home? *How warm and fuzzy.* That was something Ryan had never heard of before. Soldiers didn't come home because they were tired; they sucked it up, had a couple of beers, and went on to fight another day.

He looked around and thought of all the changes his father was walking into. There wasn't going to be much peace and quiet when old Jase got a load of what his happy little family had been up to in his absence.

***

Finally, the day, the hour, and almost the minute of Jason's triumphant return had arrived. Ryan leaned glumly against the doorway, watching his mother pin the *Welcome Home* banner over the freshly slipcovered couch.

"I am so excited," she gushed as she surveyed the decorations. "I hope he likes it."

His mom was wearing her blue-and-white flowered granny dress and her face was devoid of makeup. "He'll be here in …," she checked her watch, "exactly thirty-three minutes. And, Ryan, I don't want you to say anything to upset your dad. He's been through a lot. Let him get settled and recover from his jet lag before we launch into any bad news, past or present."

Snapping to attention, Ryan gave the Nazi straight-armed salute. "*Jawohl, mein Herr*!"

His mother was inches from his face before he

had time to blink. "Do that again, or denigrate the Canadian Forces in any way, and I will disown you as a son. *Do you understand?*"

Ryan stumbled as he reeled backward in astonishment. She turned to her decorating as though nothing out of the ordinary had happened.

He sat down hard on the chair, confusion rendering him speechless. When the car bringing his father home from the war pulled up in front of their house thirty-two minutes later, Ryan was still sitting on the chair.

The man who slowly shuffled through the doorway was almost unrecognizable. The husk of a human was stooped, and the deep lines on his face traced a road map of pain. It was the eyes that held the most startling transformation. These were not the eyes of a confident soldier, in charge and ready to make you drop and give him twenty. This man's eyes were twin black holes in the universe, from which no light escaped. Ryan didn't move as he stared at what was left of his father.

"Thank God! Welcome home, sweetheart." His mother rushed to embrace the gaunt body, but Jason remained stiff and unresponsive. "Come and sit down, dear. I've made tea. Would you like a cup?"

Jason looked at her as though he didn't understand.

"Ryan, stay with your father while I get the tea." She bustled out to the kitchen, leaving them alone.

Ryan continued to sit on the chair, trying to

think of something to say. He wished his mother would hurry up.

Jason's empty eyes travelled past Ryan to the banner proclaiming *Welcome Home, Hero!* "What's that rag for?" His voice was hoarse, as though he hadn't used it for a long time.

"Mom's invited some friends over later for a barbecue to celebrate your making it back."

For the first time since his father arrived, Ryan saw a spark in the lifeless eyes.

"No party," his father said, with none of the authority the old G.I. Jason wielded when issuing an order.

"What's that about a party?" his mom asked brightly as she came in with a tray.

Jason pointed at the sign. "Take that down. It's false advertising."

Ryan watched his mother's smile falter, then slide off her face. "If you're too tired, we can do it another time. Everyone wanted to let you know how glad they are that you're home, that's all. I'll call and cancel."

Jason sat and shakily took the teacup from his wife without drinking. "There's no hero here," he mumbled as he stared unblinkingly at something only he could see. "All I did was survive, which is not what a lot of guys did."

Ryan and his mother exchanged glances, and then both discreetly left for the kitchen.

"What was that all about?" Ryan whispered the second they were alone.

His mother's cheery bravado disappeared. "Honey, your father is ill. The doctor called to warn me that he's suffering from Post-Traumatic Stress Disorder. I didn't want to say anything until I saw for myself how he was." He could hear the strain in her voice. "He'll need all our love and help to get better."

So that explained the stranger sitting in the living room. Ryan knew nothing short of a major meltdown would have stopped Jason reading the riot act when he saw the new decorating, his mother's short hair, the mutt, or even the stupid plant sitting on its stand in plain view.

"We'll talk about this more later," his mother continued. "All I want you to do is remember that your father has a war injury just as surely as if he'd been hit by a bullet." She patted his arm as though he were a two-year-old who didn't know the score.

"Mom, for crying out loud, we live on a military base — I've heard of PTSD!"

Ryan knew about the mind crashes, depression, and flashbacks. He had read one article about a soldier with Post-Traumatic Stress Disorder who became so aggressive, they locked him up. The article had been in his gaming mag because the treatment they prescribed used virtual reality. The idea was to introduce stress a little at a time in the VR world, gradually building the guy's confidence until he could handle whatever had sent him over the edge.

His mother kept talking and Ryan wasn't sure if it was to reassure him or herself. "I don't want you to worry. I'm sure your father will be his old self soon. Now, take that gloomy look off your face and let's go have our tea."

She went back into the living room, leaving Ryan to consider this altered universe they were about to enter.

The next week was surreal. Every time Ryan saw his father, the grudging respect he'd had in the past eroded a little more, like the banks of a river at spring flood.

At first, Ryan practically tiptoed around, almost as though waiting for Jason to awake from the trance he was in. His father sat in the living room for long hours staring out the window as Ruff Cut slept at his feet. What was really bizarre was that he was in full uniform. The creases in his pants were knife sharp, and his shirt was crisp and ironed so there wasn't a wrinkle anywhere. He even wore his boots, and they gleamed in the dim light.

Then there were the nightmares. The first time that little circus happened, the whole house had panicked. Jason had started screaming in the middle of the night, yelling that he needed his weapon, that his buddies were pinned down and he had to save them. It was pandemonium. His mother frantically phoned the doctor while Ryan watched over his father as he trembled, mumbling incoherently. The doc came and did his voodoo to calm Jason while his mom hovered anxiously. No one slept after that.

Jason was like some freakazoid who sat down beside you on the subway after dark. You never knew whether the guy would detonate and try to take you out, or offer you a smoke and talk about the latest hockey scores.

His mother aged like a time-lapse picture. Her shoulders stooped and the worry lines now looked permanent.

More drugs showed up in the family medicine cabinet. When Ryan had first seen the bottle of antidepressants, he wished he could throw them and everything they represented into the garbage. It wasn't only Jason who was wrecked; all of them were affected. The drugs were a constant reminder that the iron-willed father he knew was gone. Old G.I. Jason would never have fallen back on chemicals to fix his problems.

Ryan started to think he was still the man of the house, absolutely more than the hollow shell who had returned from Afghanistan. After all, he was the Warrior Monk, a Terminator, and a force to be reckoned with.

One evening, as his mother worked late, Ryan wondered how changed Jason truly was. He decided to try a little experiment. It could cost him big, but he had to know how badly things had slipped. He walked into the living room where his father sat staring at nothing, the dog at her post by his feet.

"Hey, Jase, I want to watch some TV, and you're in my favourite chair. Why don't you sit on the couch?" Ryan waited for the explosion. Nothing. In the old days, showing that disrespect would have been grounds for a firing squad or worse. Now, his father merely got up, straightened the crease in his pants, and moved as though he didn't care where he was. The dog scratched, then followed.

Ryan felt his pulse pounding. What if this obliging easy-going Putty Man stuck around? Would that be so bad? There were some advantages — and Ryan was usually all for advantages. He didn't know if his father's new persona would last, and some part of him wasn't sure if he wanted it to. This new version was not exactly the Rock of Gibraltar, and would be a washout in a firefight, but for now, the situation was kind of exciting.

He wanted to share this with someone, someone who could appreciate the irony. He slipped into the kitchen and whipped out his phone, hitting what was still the only number other than his mother's programmed into his contact list — Casey Ardmore's. It had been days since he'd had any contact with his friend, and he was surprised when Casey answered.

"Hey, Casey, where you been? I've been trying to get a hold of you. Something wild has happened. My old man is home from the war, and he's like some kind of zombie. I'm heading to the pool at the base rec centre for a quick swim. Care to join me? I'll fill you in on all the gory details."

"Ah, things here are crazy. Can't talk right now."

Ryan heard something in Casey's voice; if he didn't know better, he would say it was nervousness. Still, he really wanted to tell HacknSlash about the new situation at home. He tried a different approach.

"Let me get this straight. You're telling me you don't want to sample some of that tasty female flesh in skimpy bathing suits? No way. I'll meet you there in half an hour."

Casey laughed, sounding more like his old self. "Yeah, what am I saying? Make it forty-five minutes."

Ryan ended the call and looked at his almost-empty cell-phone contact list. He wished he could phone Chantal and invite her along. Thinking of her made him feel bummed. He hated to admit it, but it hurt a lot when he thought of their last conversation.

"Suck it up, Warrior Monk," he chastised himself. "It's her loss." He and HacknSlash were going to the pool, where there would be lots of eligible young ladies; maybe he should pick up a girl. With his grounding gone and the word *curfew* struck from his vocabulary, this could be his night to find someone new to keep him company.

Chapter 20

Ryan leaned his bike carefully against the rack and watched Casey wheel his car into the parking lot of the rec centre. The afternoon sun glinted off Ryan's Mongoose. He had polished his bike that morning and it looked brand new. Definitely nice wheels.

"I can't remember the last time I went swimming. This is going to be insane." Casey slapped him on the back. He was twitchy, his movements spastic and uncoordinated. "Come on, Taber, you're my wingman."

Ryan frowned as he realized Casey was completely blasted. How could the guy drive when he was so wasted? It seemed being primed was HacknSlash's natural state. He had never so much as scratched that fancy car, which was a good thing, since Casey's mother was such a dragon.

Shaking his head, Ryan slung his bag across his

shoulder and they walked into the rec centre.

When Casey saw the admission charges, he scoffed. "Eight bucks! Are you kidding?"

"It's because there's a wave pool. Come on, it'll be cool," Ryan cajoled.

Casey waved his arm in dismissal. "I'm not paying that for a lousy swim."

He moved in behind a family with four boisterous children all bouncing up and down at the prospect of an afternoon playing in the artificial surf. While the clerk was dealing with the noisy group, Casey slid past the desk and walked down the hallway. He turned and gave Ryan a mock salute.

Ryan watched nervously, wanting to call him back. This was his pool, where he swam lengths and where he trained with the Sharks. He even knew the woman behind the counter. No way was he going to jeopardize that by skinning them out of a measly eight dollars.

He had a ten-swim pass and, since the woman had seen them come in together, that meant Ryan would have to use one of his precious punch-tickets to cover for Casey. Mumbling curses, he walked to the counter and paid.

The pool was filled with laughing, noisy swimmers. Ryan enjoyed it twice as much as usual since, if his mother had her way, he would still be stuck in his room pretending to do homework. There were a couple of problems when Casey decided the rules didn't apply to him and Ryan thought they were going to get turfed, but they smoothed things over with the lifeguards and got back to enjoying the waves.

Treading water as he talked, Ryan had just launched into his story about Jason's having PTSD and the bizarre things he did, when Casey cut him off. "Hey, check out that fine one in the black bikini. She looks ready, willing, and way able!" Casey, hanging on to the pool edge, whistled loudly at a pretty brunette sitting on the deck nearby. She turned away, ignoring the scene he was making.

Ryan was a little annoyed. He hadn't got to the best part about how he ordered Jason around and the old guy took it, but he knew what Casey was like when he was high and decided to humour him. "I think she's out of your league, Ardmore!"

"No way, dude. I'm going to be the best thing in that girl's universe." Casey's voice had an edge to it.

They watched appreciatively as two more tanned and extremely fit young women joined the first.

"It's turning into a smorgasbord!" Casey waved crazily, sending water splashing in all directions.

It was then that Ryan saw Hugh McAllister and a younger boy walking toward them. He almost called out, but Casey was so wasted. Ryan didn't think it was a good time for introductions.

To ensure there was no chance of an accidental meeting, Ryan struck out for the opposite side of the pool, as far away from Casey Ardmore as possible. He was strategizing like a true Terminator.

With fast, easy strokes, he reached the other side, turning in time to see Hugh wave at him. Ryan waved back as he watched the two newcomers race to the rope swing. Laughing, Hugh hip-checked his buddy into the water near where Casey was floating.

The splash was impressive; the wave hit Casey like a tsunami. Hugh, oblivious to the danger his innocent horseplay had invited, kept going. Ryan held his breath. Knowing what Casey was like on drugs, he feared what would come next.

As though he had written the script, Ryan watched the scene unfold in slow motion. Casey morphed into a creature from his worst nightmare. Furious, the Death Dealer turned on the hapless kid in the water near him. As quick as a striking cobra, Casey grabbed the young swimmer and slammed his head against the side of the pool. As the boy slumped, Casey pushed him under the water.

Ryan was stunned. This couldn't be happening. Casey had gone berserk — a broken interface; he was having a total system crash!

Arms churning the water, Ryan sped back. He shoved Casey out of the way, then dove for the unconscious boy, who was drifting to the bottom of the pool. A dark red trail spiralled ominously in the water.

Ryan pulled himself down as fast as he could,

each movement felt like lifting a tonne of weight. With agonizing slowness, he reached the boy and hooked one arm across his limp chest. The exertion had Ryan's lungs screaming for oxygen as he kicked frantically for the shimmering surface. He rose to see two lifeguards and Hugh leaning over the pool edge.

They hauled the young swimmer onto the deck and one lifeguard started CPR while the other ran to call an ambulance. The boy's skin was the colour of ashes. Hugh stood shivering nearby, a stricken look on his face.

Mesmerized, Ryan watched blood from the gash on the kid's head spread across the grey concrete deck. It filled the tiny cracks and holes, making the cement look freshly painted a violent red.

Around him, whistles blew as staff herded everyone out of the pool.

"Dude, over here ..." Casey whispered, indicating a quiet area by the waterslide.

Startled, Ryan tore his focus from the red tide to where Casey stood impatiently signalling him. He moved toward the Death Dealer. "Are you crazy? I saw what you did! I saw you smash that kid's head!"

Casey's face twisted into a mask so ferocious, Ryan froze, his breath catching.

"Shut up, punk!" Casey hissed. "You didn't see anything, got it? That bot can take the fall for this one." He pointed at Hugh.

Ryan couldn't believe what he was hearing. It was as though he was the one who had been held underwater and now had to fight for air or drown. The maniac standing in front of him was someone Ryan didn't know and, he realized with a stab, someone he didn't *want* to know. "That's really uncool. You have to go to the authorities and tell them what happened."

HacknSlash took a menacing step closer. "I'm not telling anyone anything. And neither are you."

Ryan knew he had to take a stand. "If you don't, I will. Hugh's innocent."

As he turned away, Casey put an icy hand on his arm. "Taber, you know a Death Dealer would rather die than show mercy. Remember, I know stuff that will put your head on the chopping block right alongside mine. When your mother finds out about what you've been doing, it will break her heart, especially when you end up doing time in juvie."

Ryan had no idea what Casey was talking about. He hadn't done anything serious enough to warrant jail time. What made him nervous was that he knew Casey always had a foxhole; he never left himself in the line of fire.

"You don't have anything on me, Ardmore, so stop the BS. You have to tell them you freaked out and accidentally hit the kid too hard. They'll go easy on you."

Casey sneered. "You're not listening. It's not going to be an issue, because you aren't going to say a word about this."

"We'll see about that." Ryan took a step toward the lifeguard.

"I'm sure the cops will be interested in the little video presentation I pieced together of your rise and fall. And, oh, I have a nice shot from my cell phone of you making a pickup from a known crack house ..."

Ryan's attention snapped back. "What crack house?" It took him a second, then he remembered the cell call Casey took when they were getting the track winnings. There had been an odd clicking sound, but he'd thought it was only Casey ending his call. Stupid rookie mistake. Then the full understanding of what these threats meant blasted into his brain and it took all his will power not to punch the creep in the face. "Those pickups weren't drugs. I checked."

Casey's lip twisted into a sneer. "So you opened one of the little goodie bags? Smart — I would have done the same. The problem is that you didn't go far enough. You should have opened *all* of them. Then you would have seen that one time it was cash, the next it was dope. It was a nice system, very lucrative, which was how I was able to skim a little here and there." He seemed to be talking to himself as he added, "There was so much, I didn't think anyone would mind if I took a little cut."

Ryan was furious, mostly with himself. He should have checked every damn one of those packages. He had been a trusting patsy. "You lying scumbag. I believed you when you told me that story about your mother and her betting."

Casey was enjoying himself. "That's because you're such a noob. The cops will love the tapes of you delivering dope to a dealer. You even waved. You've been running crack for months now, and there's A/V proof. Oh, I nearly forgot — as an added feature, I have some nice footage of you enjoying a little weed with Red. I have surveillance on the *inside* as well as the outside of my crib."

His tone was venomous and Ryan felt like a total fool. "How did you think that witch I call my mother could afford those wheels and the money I toss around?" Casey taunted. "We live in Welfare Row, not Buckingham Palace."

Speechless, the events replayed in Ryan's head. He should have realized what was going on. It explained so much — the car, the cash, the video cameras … He had been an idiot, totally suckered, and was now on the hook to HacknSlash for all time.

It would destroy his mom. Not to mention maybe pushing his father into some dark place he could never come back from. Casey had him cold. Death Dealer — one; Warrior Monk — zero.

Casey's eye's narrowed. "I don't want to burn you to the ground, Taber, but it's a tough game and I play to win. Go along with me and everything will work out. That bot will get off doing minimum time, and you and I will skate."

"It's always about winning the game with you, isn't it?" Ryan had to turn away before he lost it.

The pool had been cleared and the cavernous building seemed eerily quiet. Ryan watched Hugh, who stood silently waiting as staff members continued to work feverishly on the still boy.

Hugh's head came up and their eyes met. Ryan flushed and looked away as the paramedics hustled in. Moments later, the police arrived and the slim hope Ryan had that this would be chalked up to a simple swimming accident sank. He knew they would be questioned, and Casey's threats loomed large in his mind.

HacknSlash saw the officers and immediately went on the offensive.

"That guy, there," he pointed an accusing finger at Hugh. "He shoves this poor kid, who slips, see, and he hits his head as he goes into the water. Crack! Plain as day! He watched the kid bleed. Then instead of helping, this hero goes on his freakin' way. The animal left the little dude to drown."

He sounded so disgusted and so convincing that Ryan had to remind himself that it wasn't what happened.

"That's a lie! Josh was fine when he went in." Hugh protested. "I didn't hit him that hard, just a little hip-check."

The police officer eyed Hugh closely. "So you admit you hit him?"

"Yes, but, it didn't happen the way this liar

said," Hugh fixed his gaze on Casey, then a look of comprehension crossed his face. "In fact, he was the closest swimmer to Josh. He did something when Josh was in the water. You should be asking him what happened!"

The officer paused in his note-taking and looked at Casey, who was doing a great imitation of a choirboy.

Hugh became frantic. "Ryan, you saw, right? Tell them what happened. Josh cleared the deck."

The desperation in his voice was obvious and Ryan wondered if someone could go into shock from simply watching such a train wreck. "Ah, I … well, I was across the pool …" he stalled.

"I didn't do anything to the kid," Casey interrupted. "My friend Ryan can vouch for me, Officer." He emphasized *Ryan*. "We go way back and do everything together, right, Ryan?"

Ryan didn't know what to say. If he sided with Casey, that left Hugh twisting in the wind. If he told the police what had really happened, Casey would burn Ryan's world to a cold, black cinder.

Instead, he addressed the paramedics as they prepared to wheel the unconscious boy away. "Is he going to be okay?"

The paramedic looked doubtful. "We won't know for sure until we get him to the hospital. It's a good thing you were there, because a couple of seconds more and there'd be no doubt about his future."

"So he may never be able to tell you what this

criminal did?" Casey interjected, flashing a glare at Hugh.

"It's too early to say what will happen." The paramedic picked up his emergency kit, placed it on the stretcher at Josh's feet, and wheeled the portable gurney out.

The police officer turned to Ryan. "Your friend, here, says you saw what happened and he had nothing to do with the injury."

This was it. Ryan was out of time. His throat ached when he spoke. "That's right, Officer. It happened when Hugh bumped Josh into the pool." He tried to mitigate the lie. "I'm sure Hugh didn't realize he'd hurt the boy. It was an accident."

Hugh's mouth dropped open.

The policeman tucked his small notebook into his jacket and turned to Hugh. "Son, you'll have to come with me so you can make a formal statement."

Ryan stood aside as Hugh, looking pale and frightened, was led away by the burly officer.

Chapter 21

Ryan felt sick as he and Casey left the building. He knew his days with the Sharks had ended the second he sided with the Death Dealer. This wasn't about him alone, he reminded himself; there was his mom and Jason to consider. Somehow, he would have to find a way out of this nightmare.

They were walking to the parking lot when Ryan suddenly froze. "Oh, my God!"

His bike lay in a twisted, tortured heap, totally, thoroughly, utterly demolished. He felt numb as he stared at what was left of his most prized possession.

"What the …" Casey roared.

It was then that Ryan saw the silver Mercedes.

The sleek doors were caved in, the stylish fenders dented, and the pristine windshield a spidery web of smashed glass. The high-end silver paint was bubbled and ruined by what could only have been acid thrown onto the hood.

"Those sons of …" Casey cursed. "They've gone too far this time. I'll end up in a body bag when I go home."

"Casey, you told me those thugs were nothing to worry about? I'd say this," Ryan indicated the trashed bike and car, "is something to worry about." He thought of the chase when he'd barely beaten the train, and of the veiled threat the goons had made toward his mom. "You have to fix this. Do whatever it takes to get them to stop before someone gets killed."

HacknSlash paced up and down, agitatedly running his hands through his hair. "Oh, man, this sucks. Goddamn, it so sucks!" he moaned.

Casey's whole demeanour screamed defeat, something Ryan was shocked to see in the master gamer. The extensive damage on the trashed car seemed fair, considering the loss of his treasured bike.

He thought of how Casey had made him lie about Hugh, and the mangled mess of metal spread out before them was like some kind of cosmic payback. "Well, looks like we're both going to be without wheels for a while. Hey, the cops are still in the rec centre. You could get them out here and file a vandalism complaint. Of course, when they ask if you know of anyone who might want to do this," he quirked an eyebrow, "that could lead to some embarrassing questions."

Casey's moment of weakness had passed, and he turned on Ryan. "Shut up!" He strode to the ruined car, yanked a tire iron out of the trunk, and banged the splintered windshield, punching the broken glass free. Without another word, he climbed in, fired the engine, and cut out of the parking lot.

Ryan stood over his destroyed bike. It was like looking at the body of a dead friend. He thought of how hard he had worked to get it. Something his gran used to say floated into his head: *You lie down with dogs, you get up with fleas.*

Casey Ardmore had turned out to be one bad-ass dog.

***

After disposing of the bike carcass, Ryan started the long march home. Tired and dejected, he walked into his house to find his father still sitting where Ryan had left him hours before.

Where was the strong, forceful soldier who always knew exactly what to do when things went wrong? What had happened to the man who ran their ship with an iron fist? Here was the one time in his life when he could have used G.I. Jason's straight-ahead, drill-sergeant approach, and the guy had gone AWOL! Without a word, Ryan pounded upstairs to his room and slammed the door.

When his mother came home, Ryan remained

in his room, unable to face her. Would she pay for his screw-up? He had a flash of the acid-burned car. Would Hugh have to take the fall because Ryan didn't have the guts to step up? He didn't know what to do, and he was scared.

For the next week, Ryan holed up in his room, telling his mother he was sick. He didn't go to school — why bother? He stayed away from the CyberKnights Café; the goons might be lurking. Worst of all — he passed on the Sharks. He wondered how Hugh was doing and felt his guts constrict.

He didn't eat, abandoned sleep, and felt gross all the time. Try as he might, he couldn't get that poor Josh kid out of his head. A couple of times he dozed, only to be haunted by a ghost of a body drifting in the still water of the pool.

His mom started up with the mother hen routine the second day into his self-imposed exile, offering to take him to the doctor, asking what was wrong, and even making him a cliché bowl of chicken soup.

When Coach Kraus called, Ryan could hardly bring himself to answer the phone.

"Because of what happened, it would probably be best if you stayed away until this is cleared up. Joshua is still in a coma and Hugh is facing charges of assault causing bodily harm." There was a pause on the line. "Ryan, he swears he didn't hurt Josh, and says you could have cleared him. Can you tell me what happened?"

Ryan swallowed the bile rising in his throat. The words were on the tip of his tongue, words that would clear Hugh, but he couldn't do it until he had a way of ensuring the right guy was charged. He needed time. "I'm sorry, Coach. I guess Hugh should have made sure Josh was okay after he went in."

The coach said he would stay in touch. Ryan figured there was no hope of that happening. He was on his own. If a solution was going to be found, it was up to him.

The problem was that he had screwed up so badly, he wasn't sure he could figure a way out. He remembered all the low-life things he had done, the guilt oozing like pus from a putrefying sore. A kaleidoscope of ugly images flooded his brain: Hugh's desperate pleas; Josh being wheeled away; treating his classmates and teachers like losers; smoking and cutting class; the constant lying to his mom; and, he realized guiltily, the worst was the way he had treated Jason. Then he thought of Chantal and, as low as he felt, he managed to slip down even further. Yeah, he sucked.

How could he fix this mess? The answer was obvious — he had to get Casey to confess. The question was, *how*?

Chapter 22

It was late Friday night when Ryan's cell phone began jangling insistently. He lay on his bed, one arm flung over his eyes to shut out as much of the world as possible. Since there were only two people in the known universe who had his number, and one was walking her dog right now, Ryan knew who was calling. Rolling over, he flipped open the phone. "What do you want, Casey?"

"I've got a problem, and I ... I need your help. This is a matter of life or death, bro. I'm talking serious shit."

He sounded so strung-out and desperate it shocked Ryan. Casey Ardmore was in trouble he couldn't wipe off on someone else. Well, surprise, surprise!

Ryan was about to tell him to take a hike when it hit him — this could be his opportunity, the very one he needed. Somehow, he had to persuade

Casey to go to the police, and helping him might give him the leverage to make that happen. He had to find out more. "So, why call me?"

"Things are tense. It's those losers." There was an audible sigh on the other end of the line. "Okay, okay, the truth is, I used to be their runner and I ripped them off for a pile. The money's gone and there's no way I can pay them back. They said they're going to make an example of me. I need to get out of town now, but I think the Greyhound here is being watched. You have to take me to the bus station in Leduc. It's only twenty minutes out of Edmonton."

Casey's voice was shaking. Ryan knew he had to figure a way to use this to his advantage — and fast. "I don't have a car and, thanks to you, I don't even have my bike anymore," he stalled. "How am I supposed to ferry you all the way out there?"

"Your mother has a car, doesn't she?"

"Yeah, so?"

"So, boost it. This is an emergency."

It was so typical. Casey had a problem, so Ryan was expected to bust every law to accommodate. "Why don't you take a cab? You're always rolling in money."

Casey's voice was bitter. "The rotten Hag cancelled my credit cards and cleaned out any money I had stashed to pay for her trashed car. I barely have enough for bus fare, and none of my other so-called friends are anywhere to be found."

Ryan liked what he heard. Casey was on the

receiving end of trouble for a change, and it gave Ryan a big hammer to swing, one he wasn't afraid to use. Until he thought of exactly how to use this hammer, he couldn't let HacknSlash disappear. "Where do you want to meet?"

Some of the old confidence returned to the gamer's voice. "Be at CyberKnights in fifteen minutes. Don't bail on me, Taber."

"Oh, I'll be there. One more thing." Ryan heard Casey hesitate on the other end of the phone.

"What?" Casey asked tentatively.

"Bring the tapes and your cell phone." Ryan couldn't believe what he was doing. He was shaking down the king of shakedowns.

Casey snickered. "Don't be such a clown. Do you think I have only one copy of the footage of you misbehaving? Any Death Dealer worth his hard drive would cover his flanks."

Ryan could have slapped himself for such an amateur gambit. Of course Casey would have backups, and now Ryan had tipped his hand. "Can't blame a guy for trying," he laughed, shooting for nonchalant.

Ryan raced downstairs and pulled on his jacket, then reached into his mom's backpack to retrieve the car keys. It had started to rain and he knew his mom would be back with her furry hound any minute. If his plan was going to work, he had to be fast.

He looked at his father and stopped. He thought of the way he had treated Jason, and knew he had a lot to make up for. This man was broken, and instead of helping, Ryan had sunk to a level where the strong preyed on the weak, using and abusing before destroying.

Lines as deep as badlands canyons etched his father's tired face. His hair, which had grown considerably, was shot through with grey. Ryan tried to remember if it had been that way before he went to Afghanistan. Ryan didn't know what had happened to bring about this change, still he knew he had to make sure he didn't add to the burden. "I have to go out for a little while."

His father turned to him, eyes emotionless, dull. He had started some new meds, and Ryan wondered if they were helping or making things worse.

"I'm borrowing the car. Tell Mom not to worry. I'll explain everything later. I have to do this; it's important. You got that, Dad?" he asked gently.

His father's brow furrowed. "Car? Right, I'd forgotten the car." The furrow turned to a frown. "*You* are taking the car?"

Ryan headed for the door before the conversation took a wrong turn. There was no way he could explain things now.

More than a little nervous, Ryan aimed the car in the general direction of the café. He had played Formula One and Track Day race games at the arcade, but this was different. Watching for other cars, road signs, and traffic lights; signalling and keeping to the speed limits — driving was way more complicated than he thought. He used to play a tank commander game that required coordinating a lot of different skills, and this was kind of like it, only now there would be mega-serious consequences if he hit anything.

By the time Ryan turned in to the parking lot, he had gained a little confidence, his hands relaxed a little on the wheel, and he decided driving was something he could really enjoy. Satisfied with his first solo flight, he locked the car and started into the familiar hangout. His sense of well-being dried up when Casey stepped out of the shadows.

Casey's face was sweaty. "Did anyone follow you?" he asked, furtively checking the street.

"Of course not," Ryan scoffed with a false bravado. "I'm no rookie." In fact, he had been too preoccupied with the rules of the road to notice anything except the colour of the traffic lights. "Are you sure *you're* alone?" he shot back. Since he still hadn't come up with a master plan for the whole *Casey-confesses-to-the-cops* thing, he had to try to stall until something workable struck him. He swiped at the rain dripping down his face. "Let's go inside."

"Are you whack?" Casey shouted. "I don't want to waste a minute more in this hole. There's a six o'clock bus for Calgary with my name on it."

"Ah, actually, I've been thinking about what happened at the pool …" Ryan hesitated as he tried to find the right words. "And I've decided

157

you have to go to the cops and tell them the truth. You can't hang Hugh out to dry for something you did, then bug out."

Casey looked at Ryan as though he had lost his mind. "*You've decided?* You really are an idiot. If you recall, we already had this conversation. It went something like this: not only am I *not* telling the cops anything, *neither are you*. I'm gone before those Neanderthals figure out what I'm doing, and you're going to help me. After that, you'll keep your mouth permanently shut about anything we've done together, or the cops will score big time in the evidence department and we'll both go down."

Casey took a step closer. "You seem to forget, you went along with hanging the pool thing on your buddy. If I remember rightly, you even *lied* to a cop, which might make it hard for them to figure out when you're telling the truth. And don't kid yourself. I'll make sure your family knows all the dirty details about your sordid playtime activities. I'm sure that will give them nightmares for years."

It was at that precise moment that Ryan's world crashed around him, and the thin wire he had been walking on since he met Casey Ardmore snapped.

All this time, Ryan had looked up to the guy, but now he saw that Casey was no hero. He doubted the guy could function in normal society. It stung that this was probably why the Death Dealer had hung with him; Casey didn't fit in with ordinary people, only cybermonkeys who lived in the imaginary world of e-games like *Desert Death*.

The attention the cybergod lavished on Ryan had clouded his judgment, morphed him into some kind of toxic poison. He had gone along with Casey and his lies for too long. Now, that was all finished.

It was time to make a difference. He needed help, but what? How? His hand slipped into his pocket and his fist tightened around his mother's car keys. As he stared at the glowing neon sign above the café door, a desperate plan bubbled up in his mind. It was completely insane, not to mention nearly impossible, and Ryan was scared to calculate the odds it would work. Still, he had no choice.

With a sense of calm he hadn't felt for months, Ryan smiled at the Death Dealer. "I've got a proposition that will make your day."

"Yeah, what?" Casey asked suspiciously.

"How'd you like a set of wheels to take you anywhere you want?" Ryan pulled out the keys and held them up, the red light glinting off the shiny metal. "My wheels are way better than yours, because the knee-breakers don't have the faintest what this car looks like. You could slide right past them and they wouldn't have a clue."

Casey's eyes glittered as if lit from inside. "I like it." He reached for the glowing keys.

Ryan snatched them back at the last second.

"Not so fast, and not so easy. I said I have a *proposition* for you. Here's the deal. We have a high-stakes game of *Desert Death*. If I win, we go to the cops and tell them everything; if you win, you get these keys and as long a head start as I can give you before my mother or those gorillas catch up with me."

He watched Casey, and it was as if he could hear the gears turning. Ryan had played the gamer long enough to know that the chance was an irresistible draw for him. The only problem was that Ryan had never beaten the master before.

A twisted laugh gurgled from HacknSlash's throat. "It's your funeral."

Chapter 23

The loud beat of the techno music slammed Ryan's ears as he followed Casey into the deep recesses of the dimly lit café.

"I'll network our computers, then we're going to change it up a bit." HacknSlash dropped his coat on the back of the chair. "Surprise! I'm going to jump to the other side and fight for the Nomads in our little death match. As a Defender, you can try to hammer me, which should suit your goody-two-shoes mentality."

Ryan stopped dead in his tracks. As far as he and the rest of cyberspace knew, it was impossible to be a Nomad fighter. That was the way the guy who wrote the program planned it, and that was one of the reasons he liked *D-Death* so much.

Then something from a long-ago conversation rang a bell. When they first met, Casey said a *higher power* had taken over the bots in the skirmish Ryan lost. At the time, Ryan had dismissed it as gaming-babble.

"You're telling me you've hacked *Desert Death*?"

This was heavy-duty stuff. It would be an amazing feat, and would also allow HacknSlash to skew things in his favour, which meant all his scores were in the tank. If this got out, he'd be finished in the gaming universe.

Ryan watched as the cybermaster calmly keyboarded, as though admitting he corrupted the game was an everyday thing. It seemed he had not just rewritten the game, he felt he *was* the game and could do what ever he wanted. "I've never liked boxes, so I *finessed* the program a little. HacknSlash is the name; code-breaking is the game." His voice was smug. "It was a steep challenge, way past cheats or Easter eggs. As you know, this game practically learns as it plays, adapting to changes and strategies as the combatants go on. My modifications let me decide what rules to run, which includes fighting as a Nomad if I want. Tonight, *I want*." He glanced slyly at Ryan. "Still in, Taber?"

Ryan prayed he was up for the challenge. "I'm going to whup your Nomad ass so bad, you'll be crying for mercy. And, HacknSlash, one more thing …" Casey turned to him and Ryan drew himself up. "In here, the name's *Warrior Monk*."

***

The game launched with a bang as an IED exploded beside the Humvee Warrior Monk and his squad were riding in. Having a six-man team was another of Casey's adaptations, and team-playing was a new experience for Ryan. When he played, he lived in the game, and it made him nervous to be responsible for the other men, even if they were bots. The bomb put their vehicle out of action and injured two of his men, but the other four were able to go on. Ryan ordered one man back, a rifleman who was also a medic, to look after the injured soldiers. He had only been playing five minutes and his firepower had already dropped dramatically. On the other hand, leaving help for the wounded made his Ethical Rating take a big jump.

Both he and Casey had reviewed topographical and geographical maps of the zone they were playing in, not to mention picked their armaments and team members. The objective was for Warrior Monk to capture or kill the leader of the Nomads — cut off the head and the rest of the beast would fall. He couldn't win by simply chasing HacknSlash until he cornered him, as the Nomad leader would be trying to take out Warrior Monk at the same time. Ryan knew HacknSlash would sacrifice everything and anyone to win. He had seen how the gamer loved fatalities — ripping out a spine or heart with his bare hands was Casey's idea of a sweet victory.

The map showed that the only defensible position for the Nomads was in the distant mountains, and Warrior Monk and his squad battled their way across the arid desert terrain toward this goal. He not only had to keep his men as safe as possible, no cannon fodder allowed. He also had to make sure they had food, water, and rest, or the computer would penalize him.

HacknSlash was completely focused as Ryan sneaked a surreptitious look his way.

In that instant, a rocket exploded near Ryan's patrol, taking out their communications man and their link to HQ. "Stupid, stupid, stupid!" He had lost focus and it had cost him. Quickly, he redirected his remaining two troops to more cover.

In the distance, the pass they were moving through narrowed, and Ryan saw two spots that were perfect for a Nomad ambush. The question was which one had the master gamer chosen?

Casey's eyes sparked fire in the light from the screen. Countless losing contests had taught Ryan that the Death Dealer anticipated fresh blood.

Almost as an afterthought, Ryan noticed a tank carcass lying derelict at the side of the road, exactly like dozens of others his short-handed patrol had passed. Then the hair on the back of his neck prickled. He had only two heavy-armour-piercing shells. If he was wrong, it would cost him huge, but if he was right ... He targeted the wrecked tank and fired.

His body count jumped by four; the eliminated Nomad fighters lay dead on the sand. Ryan's score went up several hundred points.

Casey's mouth twisted. "Lucky guess."

Ryan studied the screen, cataloguing every detail.

The battle raged, and several times Ryan had to choose between losing ground or sacrificing a man. There was no way he would give HacknSlash the satisfaction of taking one more of his squad, so he fell back. At one point, he was forced to use his last heavy ordnance to blast a car making a suicide run. Again, kill points were registered, however the HacknSlash avatar hadn't been one of the slain.

The Nomads were savage, showing no mercy, and HacknSlash's hand was obvious in their programming.

Warrior Monk and his men approached a bombed-out village. Even to Ryan's practised eye, the amount of carnage seemed excessive. He moved his men in with particular care.

They approached the wreckage of a ruined building and, when Ryan checked inside, found five civilian casualties. He figured HacknSlash's ER must be taking a beating for killing the innocent. A child with a bloody leg blown apart by shrapnel lay twitching, and Ryan had no choice; he had to stop and render aid. His squad was due for a rest break anyway, so it worked out well. They moved in.

Without warning, a huge explosion sent Ryan reeling. The point soldier closest to the injured child was turned into pulpy fragments as the bomb concealed in the kid's toy detonated.

Casey laughed out loud. "And then there were two!"

Ryan's heart raced as the deadly toll registered on the stats board. He glimpsed a shallow depression in the flat field up ahead, and the last two fighters sprinted for the meagre cover, strafing as they went.

He surveyed the terrain and saw the craggy mountainside rising above them. The cliffs were riddled with caves and other natural cover for the Nomads. Ryan realized it would be impossible to corner the elusive desert fighters on their home turf. Checking the clock on the computer, he saw it was late afternoon in the scenario, and would soon be dark. This would work perfectly for the Nomads, as Warrior Monk and his remaining trooper couldn't possibly watch for ambush from every direction at once.

The shadows altered in the game, simulating fading light conditions in the battle scene. It would be a long night — or worse, an extremely short one.

Ryan had to change the odds to his favour. He desperately needed reinforcements. Waiting until the sun was low on the horizon, so his man would have as much help from poor visibility as possible, he ordered the trooper to HQ for help. Warrior Monk remained, trying to cover the hundred black openings in the cliff.

The soldier had barely begun sprinting back

from the foxhole when there was a sickly *thunk!* He lay sprawled on the ground, a splash of red marking the hit. The computer showed a sniper had wounded, not killed, Ryan's last bot.

"Now what will you do, loser?" Casey taunted. "There'll be no cavalry riding in to rescue your sorry ass."

Ryan's mouth was dry and his hands tingled from the tension. He had to do something. He couldn't leave his man out there for the buzzards. Moving was a bad option. HacknSlash would take him down and it would be game over.

Casey would win everything.

He studied the scores of caves where the master gamer had chosen to make his stand. He had no idea if HacknSlash was alone or if a horde of Nomads waited. Ryan couldn't possibly cover all the sniper positions. Add the fact that he had only one round left, and the answer was obvious — he was history.

Besides, even if the numbers were even and there were only two desert fighters left, Ryan had at best a fifty-fifty chance of winning. Ryan had to kill the avatar representing HacknSlash to end the game.

Every detail was burned into his memory. He had come so far, and knew this was Hugh's last chance to be cleared. Sweat ran down the shallow gully of his spine as he prayed for a sign. The wounded man on the ground moaned and Ryan cursed. HacknSlash would shoot the soldier again, probably in the leg, torturing both Ryan and the bot, and forcing Ryan into the open for the rescue. It was Casey's style.

If Ryan chose to leave his man out there, his Ethical Rating would tank and continue to drop for each minute the guy languished. He had two choices. Make a mad, foolish dash to rescue his fallen comrade, which would probably get him killed, or use his last bullet to shoot the trooper himself. He would take a serious hit in his ER if he chose the second course of action, but he would stop the continued drain on his reserves incurred by leaving the bot out there. He still had his knife, and maybe HacknSlash would want to finish him with some hand-to-hand. He might be able to take him.

Back in the old days, before Casey had taught him to kill first and ask questions later, 'nading his own man to save his butt hadn't been Ryan's way. And now that he was ditching everything else he had been taught by Casey, his Killing Field style of playing should go too.

Ryan thought of Jason. They had never seen eye-to-eye on much, but the one thing they did agree on was that the Tabers don't leave a man behind. Ryan readied himself to make a run for the injured soldier, and hoped he could drag him back to the foxhole before HacknSlash or one of his minions got off a lucky shot.

Warrior Monk darted for his man, closing the ground between himself and the injured bot. A furious storm of bullets proved the odds too low. Ryan could have sworn he actually felt the round hit when his avatar fell to the ground.

Injured, no kill, the computer registered.

Great! Ryan's avatar lay on the ground waiting for HacknSlash to finish him off. A bullet whizzed past and slammed into the soldier Ryan had been trying to rescue. The trooper's head blossomed into a crimson mass.

"That will seriously hurt your ER, my friend." Ryan growled as he resigned himself to the impending end. There was a reason Casey Ardmore, aka HacknSlash, was the best. He was unstoppable.

Something glinted on the screen and Ryan blinked. Had he really seen it, or was it a figment of his imagination, a game glitch? The last rays of the late afternoon sun shone on the black mouths of the caves peppering the hillside. Was someone hiding in that entrance halfway up the slope?

Warrior Monk's rifle, with his last round, lay by his side. Ryan's mind flashed back to another building in a long-ago game, in which he had reacted to a similar glint off a gun barrel. He thought of his father's e-mails, and the different strategies in the stories he used to tell him. Some had been brilliant, some had been disastrous. In all, the men had never given up, no matter what. Ryan wasn't about to go down until he had exhausted every possible gambit.

He swung the barrel and sighted on the precise

spot where he had seen the flash. He took a deep breath and held it as he pulled the trigger on his simulated rifle.

In that instant, another muzzle flash lit the dark cave. Ryan winced as he saw the computer image of his avatar slump, taking a kill shot to the heart.

The screen exploded in a shower of stars and bright flashes of light. A message appeared in blood red letters:

NEW DEATH DEALER IN THE GAME!
CONGRATULATIONS, WARRIOR MONK!

New Death Dealer? That could only mean one thing. Ryan had killed the lead Nomad. *He had killed HacknSlash's avatar!* He had won!

This made no sense. His own player lay finished on the ground.

His eyes flicked to the stats on the screen. Both he and HacknSlash had been killed, with equal numbers of men dead on both sides, so why had the computer declared Ryan the winner and promoted him to Death Dealer?

Ryan read the last remaining stats.

Ethical Rating
HacknSlash: -28
Warrior Monk: +172

It was Ryan's ER that had given him the edge! The computer had declared Warrior Monk the winner based on the only stat that showed him clearly ahead.

Ryan had beaten the master gamer, fair and square! "Justice at last!" he crowed, punching the air in victory.

Casey turned on him. "I don't care what you think you've won. I'm not going to the cops, so you can forget that crap. Now, give me those keys!" Casey launched himself at Ryan, fists flying.

Caught completely off guard, Ryan felt Casey's fist connect with his jaw and a lightning bolt shot up the side of his head. He tasted blood and knew he had bitten his tongue. "Get off me, you jerk!" Ryan yelled.

Casey was a street fighter and it showed in his vicious style. He hammered Ryan, kicking and biting, landing punch after punch. All Ryan could do was try to protect his head and face.

"Break it up, you two!" Heavy hands pulled them apart.

Ryan's left eye screamed with pain, and he swung his fist in a last-ditch effort to force Casey off him. Surprise turned to shock when he connected, and then found himself looking into Eugene's startled face. "Oh, man, I'm sorry. I didn't mean to hit you!"

"This loser attacked me too!" Casey protested. "I beat him and he went psycho! First me, then you. I think he should be banned permanently."

Eugene appeared to have handled similar

situations before. He picked up an overturned chair with an unconcerned air. "Warrior Monk, you know the rules. No fighting, especially with the staff, and if you interfere with another gamer, your computer privileges are suspended. You'll have to sit the next week out." He looked around at the mess. "I'll figure out what the damages are and take it off your credits. Now, beat it!"

With surprising strength, Eugene hustled them out the door. Then he stood with arms crossed, watching through the window like a playground monitor or, Ryan thought grimly, a prison guard. Standing in the cold rain, Ryan waited to see if the attack would resume. Instead, the fight seemed to have drained out of Casey.

Ryan felt more than cheated. Casey had destroyed a sacred trust. It was an unwritten law that gamers paid their debts to other players, and that your victory or loss was acknowledged by the cybercommunity. "You lost, HacknSlash. I should have known you wouldn't stand by your word. You can come with me, or you can wait for the cops to pick you up. Either way, the truth is coming out, and I don't care what you do with your lousy tapes."

Casey sneered. "Do you think the cops will believe you? When I tell them you picked a fight with me and got tossed from your favourite hangout, they'll think you made up everything for revenge. Having that dumb bouncer in there as a witness will help."

Ryan felt like he had been kicked again. The master gamer was right. This was going to make going to the police even tougher.

Casey could smell fresh blood. "Like I said, it's your funeral, Warrior Monk."

Despite everything, Ryan's spirits lifted. "About time you got the name right." Hearing HacknSlash at last call him by his correct user name took a bit of the sting out of what had just gone down. Ryan had come this far; he wasn't going to quit on Hugh now. "I'll put my Ethical Rating up against yours any day, Ardmore. I'm going to the police and we'll let them decide the winner in this game."

The rain had eased, and there was a break in the heavy clouds that allowed a silver sliver of moonlight to shine through. Ryan straightened his shoulders and, without a backward glance, walked to the car.

As he left the parking lot, he thought he saw a dark SUV pull in.

Chapter 24

Ryan's mother and father were waiting for him at home. He watched as their faces changed from anger to serious concern at his appearance. His left eye was swollen, his lip puffy, and, with his assorted scrapes and cuts, he looked like he was the one returning from a war zone. Ryan realized, in a weird way, he was.

He knew that owning up was going to be harsh, and yet he was glad he would finally be coming clean about everything. As he stood in front of his parents, he felt the weight he had been carrying for months lift from his shoulders. "Something's happened, and I have to tell you about it."

Recovering from her shock, his mother stood and moved to the kitchen door. "First, I'm going to get you some ice for that eye, and then you can explain what's going on."

Ryan sat self-consciously by his father on

the couch.

"Dad, I want to apologize. I've been way out of line." He looked down at his bruised hands, unable to meet his father's eyes. "When you left, I kind of ran off the rails. I ditched the rules. Don't get me wrong, doing what I wanted was a blast. The problem was I had to be a different person to do that, and I've discovered I don't like that person. There's this guy, Casey Ardmore, that I've been hanging around with. I thought being like Casey, a real player, would be great. Instead all I did was turn into a cheap knock-off of a class-one jerk."

It was as though a valve had opened and Ryan couldn't shut up. He had to make his father understand. "That game I play, *Desert Death*, the one you don't like? The highest rank is Death Dealer. Man, I wanted it, but no way was that happening, and I thought it was because my body count was never high enough. Tonight I saw there's another way to win, even at a game like *D-Death*. I'm not willing to sacrifice my soul for victory in the game, and sometimes the great gods of cyberspace find a way to reward you for that. You've heard about the things I've done lately … cutting class, smoking, and lying to Mom. And, well, I'm sorry. I know I added to your worry, and it was selfish and stupid."

His mom had returned and stood silently in the doorway listening. She walked over and handed him the ice pack, then sat on the old couch next to him. He felt like a small child, a parent on each side of him.

She patted his knee. "I think you need to know something. I never told your dad about any of the trouble you got into. You were right, he had enough stress over there; I could hear it in his voice every time I spoke to him. So he doesn't know about any of the things you just confessed to."

Ryan was confused. "The punishments and the grounding, all that stuff you told me he'd deal with when he got home. You made it up?"

"Our lives were upside down. I thought that maintaining the link to your father would help things stay normal — or as normal as it gets when a family is living under this kind of tension. We may not always seem like it, but your dad and I are a team, Ryan. We stick together, and when he wasn't here, I had to step up and make the decisions. I decided you needed to know your dad was still in the game." She raised an eyebrow. "You seemed to be having some growing pains, a little difficulty making wise choices."

"Your mother did the right thing. Still, it sounds like you and I should have a long talk." His dad's voice was gentle, but the look he gave Ryan was almost like the old G.I. Jason. For the first time, Ryan had a flash that his dad, or maybe a softer version, might come back to them.

"Yeah, I guess," he agreed. "Right now, I have to tell you both something, and then I need your help, because I have to go to the police and they may not believe me."

At the mention of the police, both his parents looked surprised. Ryan told them the whole gruesome story, including the night's activities and the wager of his mother's car against Casey confessing about the pool incident. When he said the police may think he made up the story for revenge, he saw his father's jaw tighten, an old gesture Ryan was familiar with. When he finished, he sat back and waited for the explosion.

Instead, his parents exchanged a look, and it was if some unspoken words passed between them. His mom nodded imperceptibly, and his father reached out and took Ryan's hands in his big, calloused ones.

It was such an unfamiliar gesture that Ryan was taken aback. Then his father spoke, his voice choked with emotion. "Son, before we go on, I want you to understand why I came home. When I was in Afghanistan, something happened, something so terrible I thought I would never recover." He trembled as he continued. "I was on guard duty one night, and we'd had a lot of reports of an increase in suicide bombers, so we were told not to take any chances. I was sure my checkpoint was going to be targeted. It was pitch dark and a woman was walking toward me. The shape of her burka looked strange and I told her to halt. She said something I couldn't understand and she kept walking toward me. I yelled at her to stop again.

She kept coming."

Ryan looked into his father's face and saw unshed tears glistening in his eyes.

"I had only seconds to make a decision. My buddies were asleep in the tents behind me. I couldn't take the chance, I couldn't gamble with their lives. And my orders were to protect our perimeter at all costs. I shot her."

Ryan could only imagine what it took for his father to do that. "She was going to blow up you and the other soldiers in the barracks. You had to do it."

His father's voice was strangled. "Ryan, she wasn't a suicide bomber. She was pregnant, and was coming to the Canadians because our doctors had told her they would help when her time came. I killed her and her unborn baby."

Ryan saw the scene in his mind and it was horrible. It wasn't a computer-generated scenario. It had been real. He felt sick. This 24/7 soldier, this man who always lived by the rules, who always made sure everything was done by the book, who didn't make mistakes, had killed an innocent woman.

"I am so sorry, Dad. I am so very sorry." Ryan's words seemed pitifully inadequate.

His father put an arm around him. "Afterward, I guess I had a breakdown. I couldn't function. Now I think I'm getting better. What you told me tonight took a lot of guts, and that's why I thought you were man enough to hear what had happened to me. I'm proud of you for standing up to that punk. We all have to make choices about what's right and wrong, and sometimes, no matter which choice we make, there are terrible consequences. If you can make it right for Hugh, then you're a better man than this Ardmore will ever be."

"What do you want to do now?" his mother asked.

Ryan shrugged, knowing he didn't have to frag Casey. Sooner or later, Casey would do that to himself. He would cross some other druggie, or the goons would get him, or maybe the cops would pick him up. It was Casey's game, and he would have to play it out to the end. Right now, Ryan had his own demons to deal with.

"I'm going to the police and tell them exactly what I told you. Then I'll phone Hugh and apologize."

"Do you think Ardmore will come in voluntarily?"

His dad's question brought back the fleeting image Ryan had seen as he left the parking lot. If that vehicle had been the spine-twisters', then Casey might already be in a world of hurt. If he managed to get away, police custody might not seem like a bad place to be.

"What Casey does isn't important; it's what I do that counts." Ryan stood. "I'm ready. Will you come with me?" His voice faltered.

"Of course we're with you, Soldier," his dad assured him. "You and I both know that Tabers don't leave a man behind."

Ryan felt his world coming back, but it had shifted. The people around him were different and so was he.

His mother, no longer the mousy mom he had thought her to be, had become a strong and independent woman. Or maybe that other woman had been there all the time, waiting for the call to duty.

His hard-nosed father had gone to war, only to find that the rules he based his life on didn't exist. The consequences had been devastating, even when he did what a good soldier should and followed orders.

Ryan had made the biggest discovery of all about himself. He now felt part of a larger picture, where no one is so special that he can put themselves ahead of those around them. He had learned that, without rules, chaos is king. And until he was wise enough to make his own, he was content with the rules he had here at home.

He looked at his parents and they both seemed so ordinary, like any other family in the world. "I understand war differently now," he blurted, searching their faces. "War is not a game with a bunch of electronic circuits; it's living people fighting and dying for what they believe in. War shatters every life it touches, inside and out. I like this world, the real world, I mean. It's way cooler than my imagined one in cyberspace."

Ryan's mother looked at him skeptically. "Can I quote you on that?"

"Okay, okay, I know I could never give up gaming entirely. Life is going to be different around here though," he smiled at his dad. "And that's okay with me."

Everything in balance. Hadn't Chantal mentioned she wanted to learn how to ride a bicycle? Maybe he could borrow a couple from the neighbour's kids and give her a lesson or two. Who knows, it might be a new beginning for their friendship.

It was time.

He held out the car keys to his mother. "I suppose you'll want to drive?"